# My Sister Is a Dog

## Ali Sparkes

Stairwell Books //

Published by Stairwell Books
161 Lowther Street
York, YO31 7LZ

ISBN: 978-1-913432-66-9
p5

To my own Willow. If only you could read...

# Chapter 1

## In the Gutter

Joe was having a pretty average day until next door's dog tried to kill him.

It all happened very quickly. He'd nearly got to his gate and was just finishing up the jam doughnut he'd bought on the way home when he heard old Mrs Ellis from next door yelling: 'WILLOW!! GET BACK HERE! GET BACK!'

The next thing he felt was two paws whacking onto his shoulder blades. He spun around, dropping his school bag and fending off the big woolly creature as it bounced into his face.

'Get DOWN!' he shouted, but the dog appeared to have an inbuilt pogo stick and just couldn't stop itself boinging into his face. He spun away from it, turning his back so it dropped down again and that was when things went from bad to worse.

The dog pogoed into the road… just as a car went by. The driver put on the brakes with a screech and Joe realised the dog was going to bounce right into its path. He swiped for the creature's collar, hauled it back with a microsecond to spare… and then lost his balance and fell off the kerb.

The fall seemed to last a very long time. About half way down, in slow motion, he saw the dog leap right up and over his head in a graceful arc, its tail waving like a furry flag, the undersides of its paws like black pebbles, and then he saw the gritty surface of the road heading for his face and, in the corner of his eye, the gleaming metal grille of the car getting closer and closer.

He landed face-first on the road, to the sound of more screaming from Mrs Ellis and the terrifying squeal of brakes.

A big, final thud should have followed. Probably the last sound he would hear.

But it didn't. By some miracle, the driver had braked hard enough and soon enough to come to a stop about two centimetres from Joe's nose.

For a few seconds Joe lay in the road, his cheek pressed against the cold grit, gazing at the zig-zag patterns in the tyre which had so nearly rolled over his head. There was a moment of silence... a kind of anti-crash. A whiff of hot oil wafted warmly from under the car. Then a woolly body thumped down next to him and a cool nose nuzzled his ear. He rolled over to stare into the dark eyes of the dog. It peered down at him, its long ears forming a little tent between its face and his own; a small, private, furry world. Its breath smelt of cucumber.

'Are you trying to kill me?' asked Joe.

The dog licked his nose.

Then it was snapped away as Mrs Ellis and her son came to get it on the lead. Mrs Ellis was crying and apologising and the driver of the car was sitting on the kerb, holding his head in his hands and taking long slow breaths while yet another

2

person, Jed, from next door, got down on his knees to check whether Joe was dead or alive.

'It's OK,' Joe said, sitting up. 'I'm fine.'

'Easy now – easy!' said Jed. 'Don't get up. You might have hurt your neck. And you're bleeding.'

'No, really – I'm fine,' said Joe, getting to his feet. 'The car didn't hit me. And most of that is… jam. I was eating a doughnut.' He was more concerned about the driver, who was breathing very fast, and Mrs Ellis, who was still crying and scolding the dog. 'It's OK,' he said, to the driver. 'You braked really brilliantly. You saved my life.' The man looked up at him, pale and shaky. 'I live just here,' said Joe. 'Do you want to come in and have some sweet tea or something?'

The man blinked a few times and then nodded. 'Come on,' said Jed. 'Let's all go inside for a sit down and a cuppa. I'm sure Juliet won't mind.'

They got the man to his feet and walked him to Joe's front door. Over the fence, Mrs Ellis was still crying. 'It's OK!' Joe called over. 'Really! I'm fine!'

'No thanks to her!' wailed the old lady. Jed, her grandson, looked embarrassed as the head and paws of the big black dog suddenly appeared over the fence. It was panting and lolling its tongue about as if it was having a great laugh at all the mayhem it had caused. Its furry face was just under the For Sale sign that had gone up yesterday; high on a post driven in to the corner of Joe's front garden. 'You stay put!' went on Mrs Ellis, glancing up at the sign. 'Or we'll put you up for sale!'

'I'll park your car, mate,' said Jed to the shaken driver. 'And I'll lock it and bring your keys in.' The driver nodded as Joe opened the front door.

'Mum!' Joe called. 'Can we put the kettle on? A man nearly ran me over and he's in shock.'

# Chapter 2

## All About Love

Look, sometimes I have to misbehave. Sometimes I have a good reason. And it wasn't just because he smelt of jam. Although I do love jam.

I have long legs. I can easily jump over the gate. The only reason I don't is that I try to do as I'm told. Sometimes. Most of the time. And I know I will get into BIG trouble if I jump over the gate. Should I jump over the gate? Should I get into trouble?

I get up and lean on the gate and watch the back of him as he wanders down the road. He has pale hair, not at all like my dark fluffy, curly stuff. It flops forward over his eyes, which are blue. His skin is pale and a bit freckly. He's got a great, wide smile. Not that I've seen that in a long time. I would like to see it again.

Before I even know I've done it, I've leapt over the gate and I'm following him down the road. I can't help it. There are some things I cannot help. I cannot help biting cardboard. I cannot help bouncing. I cannot help loving people. I love people so much they sometimes fall over. Three things happen after I jump over the gate.

1.  Granny starts screaming.
2.  A horn goes off.
3.  Joe ends up face down in the road, under a car.

I think this may all be my fault. But I am misunderstood.

I am all about love.

It's true. All I want is to love people. They come to me smiling and holding out their hands and I leap to be with them. I leap with love.

Some of them laugh and leap back at me. But some of them shriek and flap and shout. And when that happens, I realise they are confused and they do not understand that I am all about love. So I try harder to tell them, face to face. And then they shriek and flap and shout even more.

The man who put the wooden post in Joe's garden was like that. He put a sign at the top of the post. It was right by the fence and it all was so interesting I just had to jump up. I only wanted to say hello but he went very flappy and started shouting and I had to go indoors. I just wanted to share a little happy... but some people cannot be told.

I have three things I must do. Really important things.

First – I need to let Joe know about me. I really do. Once he understands, he'll be fine. I think he nearly understood when we were both on the road. I booped him on the nose and looked into his eyes and for a moment... but then Granny and Jed were back and I had to sit and be a good girl, even though they were telling me how bad I was. Make your mind up, people. It's not just me that gets this. Zing, Bert and Loki – they all have similar problems. People don't make sense like dogs do. They are so mixed up. Here's an example. When I was little, it was all about poo.

Day 1: I pooed on the carpet. I was a Bad Girl.

Day 2: I pooed on the kitchen floor, on some paper. I was a Very Good Girl.

Day 3: I pooed on the kitchen floor, on some paper. I was a Good Girl.

Day 4: I pooed out in the garden. I was a Very, Very Good Girl.

Day 5: I pooed on the kitchen floor, on some paper.  I was not good or bad.

Day 6: I pooed out in the garden. Good Girl.

Day 7: I pooed on the kitchen floor (there was no paper). Bad Girl.

Day 8: I pooed out in the garden. **NO - NOT on the grass!** BAD Girl! **OVER HERE! On the CONCRETE!**


Oh right. So it's right one day and wrong the next! What is going on here? What's the pattern? IS there a pattern? Are we all making this up as we go along?!

DAY 9: I pooed on the carpet, the kitchen floor and in Jed's shoes. Just to work out a few boundaries. **BAD, BAD, BAD, BAD GIRL!**

DAY 10. I pooed only on the concrete. We never spoke of Day 9 again.

They are OBSESSED with poo. When I do it in the concrete corner I'm usually left alone, but when we're out, oh no. It's a whole other story. Whenever I make the shape and am about to drop, they suddenly stand rooted to the spot, staring at me. STARING at me.

I stare back. They look away. Then they gather it all up in a shiny bag as if it's something very precious. But they don't look happy. And they often crunch up their faces and make unpleasant sounds. As if it's BAD POO. Precious, precious bad poo.

And they say *I* am mad.

But they're OK. They love me. I think. Although Granny doesn't like to play and the way her knees smell, I understand why. And Jed isn't there very much.

Anyway, I didn't come back for them. I came back for Joe.

# Chapter 3

# Hyperventilation

The man who'd nearly run him over was called Ben. He lived about three roads away. He was around Mum's age and had short, ginger hair and a beard. His hands were still shaking five minutes after he'd sat down. Mum gave him a paper bag to breathe into.

'You're hyperventilating,' she told him as Joe poured out the tea and put some biscuits on a plate. 'Hold this paper bag tightly around your mouth and breathe into it. It'll start sucking in and out with your breaths. And your breathing will slowly calm down.'

Ben did as he was told and Joe watched, fascinated, as the paper bag began to move in and out, like the end of a party blower. Eventually it was sucked in completely flat as Ben breathed in... and by then Ben had stopped panting like that crazy labradoodle next door.

He put the paper bag down and picked up a mug of tea. 'Thank you,' he said. 'Who knew what a paper bag could do?'

'Everybody underestimates a paper bag,' said Mum.

'Thanks for the tea, Mrs... um..?' Ben went on, smiling at Mum.

'Call me Juliet,' she said, smiling back at him. 'And it's the least I could do after my son decided to throw himself under the wheels of your car.'

'It wasn't his fault,' said Ben. 'It was the dog. He was trying to save the dog.'

'You braked really well,' said Joe.

'Well, I'm trained,' said Ben, looking a little embarrassed. 'I'm a police officer,' he added. 'So I turn up at accidents all the time. Never thought I'd be so freaked out when it happened to me.'

'It's very different, I expect,' said Mum. 'But everyone's fine. Just a bit shaky, that's all.' She reached over and squeezed Joe's hand. 'Have a biscuit,' she said to him. 'The sugar will help with the shock. Then go and tidy your room. We've got viewers.'

Joe slumped over his tea. Not viewers. Not again.

'Oh... you're selling up?' Ben asked, looking a lot less shaky now.

'That's right. We're moving,' said Mum.

'Oh,' said Ben. 'Shame.'

'Yes,' said Mum. 'It is.'

Ben got up to go. 'Well, thank you for the tea. It was lovely to meet you. Hopefully next time I see you will be better... when I haven't just nearly killed your son.'

'Nearly killing my son isn't the best first impression,' agreed Mum, grinning and shaking his hand.

When Ben had gone she sat down and faced Joe across the kitchen table. 'Come on, Joe, don't look at me like that. We've talked about this. You know we can't afford to stay here any more.'

Joe stared at his tea and said nothing. He knew it wasn't Mum's fault but every time he thought about the little flat on the other side of town, his insides just crunched up. It was a much cheaper place to live and it was OK… if you didn't mind it being really small and having no garden… unless you counted the weedy paved area by the bins. He would have to change schools too.

Mum sighed and shook her head. 'Look, just… go up and tidy your room.'

Joe went up and got out of his school clothes. He left them – an oily, jammy, sugary pile – in the laundry basket in the bathroom.

On the way back across the landing he stopped and looked at the white door with the butterfly on it. From somewhere outside he heard that dog give a howl. It made his throat go tight. For the last three weeks, ever since Jed had come back to his gran's place to live and brought that mad, jumpy dog with him, everything seemed… on edge.

He sighed and went to his room. The dog howled again. Maybe it was planning its next attempt on his life.

# Chapter 4

## Feel Curls

We can feel things you can't. Nearby and across big distances. A lot of feelings are in the air, travelling on currents like massive rivers of feel. We smell the rivers and we find the feelings long before the person who is feeling the feeling arrives. And long after they have left.

We pick up messages from each other the same way, although sometimes the feelings are old and dried by the sun. We pick them up on posts and trees and in clumps of grass, where they have been left for us. Messages from our friends and our not-yet-friends and our never-will-be-friends. Whenever I stop too long to pick up messages Jed grumbles: 'Come on, Willow. We can't wait around all day while you check your pee-mail.'

OK, yes, the messages are delivered in wee and poo, but we don't have pens and paper, do we? And if we did… we would probably eat them.

Anyway, I get feelings all the time from Joe. They stream out of his bedroom window at night. They waft in feel curls from the kitchen, alongside the smells of cheese and toast and beans. They drip through the rain on grey days and run along the gutter and into the drain. They are mostly not good feelings. When I have made him understand, they will be good again.

I stand on the path that runs between our houses and keep very still.

'Willow. Why are you staring at the wall?' asks Granny, coming outside to scratch the bit between my ears.

I'm not staring at the wall. I'm picking up the feel curls from next door. I surprise myself by letting out a little howl.

'Are you sorry for what you did?' Granny says. 'Are you sorry for nearly getting that poor boy run over?'

I turn and look at her, tilting my head. She likes it when I tilt my head.

'Just don't do it again!' she says, but she's not telling me off now. She smells of kindness even though her face is stern – and she's still scratching my head. 'It's lovely having Jed come back to live with me, now my legs are giving me such trouble. I'm very fond of you, too, but you do try my patience, girl!'

I am sorry, of course. I didn't mean to get Joe nearly run over. BUT… it was good to see him up close. I MUST get to him again. There are three things to tell him. They are all important, but what's outside our gate – the smell and the colour – is probably the most important… and the hardest to explain when you don't have human words.

A bell rings and I smell new people. I hear them, too, as they walk up to Joe's door.

'Great kerb appeal,' one of them says.

# Chapter 5

## Knock It Right Through

'And this is the garden,' said a crisp voice. The estate agent, in his shiny grey suit, arrived on the patio with the couple. He waved at the garden, just in case they were unsure what a garden was.

Joe sat on the swing seat under the lilac tree and gritted his teeth. Mum was hiding in the greenhouse. They both had to stay out of the way when the estate agent brought people to look around. As the couple came outside there was a snuffling sound and Joe peered around and noticed a shiny black nose poking through a small gap in the fence. He pushed the nose back through to its own side, whispering 'Not NOW, dog!'

'Nice patio,' said the woman.

'Really ticks the boxes,' said the man.

'I prefer decking, though,' said the woman.

'You could easily put decking over the patio,' chipped in the estate agent.

'Hmmm,' said the man. 'We'll have to cost that up before we make an offer.'

Joe stared at him, stunned. An offer? Already? Surely not! Behind the fence there was a low growl.

As they went back into the house Joe couldn't help himself. He had to follow. Discreetly. Listening in.

'This is the front room,' the estate agent said as they went into the room at the front.

'It's a bit on the small side,' said the man.

'You could knock it right through,' said the estate agent. 'The wall would come down easily.'

'I'd have to have that fireplace out,' said the woman. 'I couldn't live with that fireplace.'

Joe, in the hallway, peered through at the fireplace. It was a simple brick fireplace with an iron basket for logs and coals which they used in the winter. He liked the fireplace. They roasted chestnuts on it sometimes. There would be no fireplace in the flat. No roasting of anything.

'The fireplace could come out easily,' said the estate agent.

'I'd like one of those white marble ones which go in the wall like a letterbox,' the woman went on. 'With blue flaming pebbles. Really stylish. It would have to be electric though; I can't be doing with lugging coal and logs in from the garden.'

Joe flattened himself against the downstairs toilet door as they all came out and trooped up to judge the bedrooms. On the landing they looked up. 'Loft access,' said the estate agent. 'For the loft.'

'Bathroom needs gutting,' said the man, as soon as the estate agent had told them it was a bathroom. (Joe had a mental image of the bath and the sink and the toilet being dragged out of the room on a massive hook and flung across the landing.) 'We'd need to get a power shower in there. And a proper Jacuzzi corner bath.'

They went into Mum's room next and he found himself creeping up the stairs to listen. 'Bay window is lovely,' said the woman. 'But honestly – the curtains!' She giggled and Joe tried to work out what could possibly be wrong with Mum's curtains.

They didn't seem to notice him as they walked back past the white door and straight into his room. It was tidy in there; he knew – he'd had to tidy it before he went to school. It had pale blue-green walls and a pattern of seaweed drifting up from the skirting board. They'd all made the seaweed shapes by dipping their hands in green paint and splodging them straight onto the walls. They'd painted crabs and fish and seahorses too. The carpet was a sandy colour – like a seabed.

'Oh dear,' said the woman. 'We'll have to paint over all that mess.'

There was a commotion at the front of the house. Shouting and… growling. Growling and barking.

Joe shot downstairs and out through the front door. Over the fence he saw Mrs Ellis, yelling at Willow.

Willow had leapt right over the fence, into their garden, and was attacking the For Sale sign. She was growling ferociously, biting it and scratching at it with her thick black claws.

'What's going on?' yelled the estate agent, bursting out through the front door behind Joe. 'What is that dog doing?! That sign is Top Move's property, that is!'

'

'WILLOW! STOP!' shouted Mrs Ellis but Willow didn't stop. With her flag-like tail waving delightedly, she leapt up and gripped a corner of the flimsy plastic sign between her teeth, tugging it over at an angle. Joe ran to get a hold of her red collar, but she kept biting the sign.

'Get your dog under control,' bawled the estate agent. Then he suddenly remembered he had house viewers with him and took a breath, forced a smile over his face, and said: 'I mean… I'm sure he's a lovely boy, a good boy, normally… just a little excitable.'

'She's a MENACE,' sobbed Mrs Ellis. 'I'm so sorry.'

At this point Willow proved how much of a menace she was by jumping up and whacking the teetering sign with both front paws. It fell on Joe's head.

'Oh no… oh no, oh no…' whimpered the woman, clinging to her husband's arm as Joe sat, dazed, in the grass. 'We can't have a dangerous dog next door… we're planning to have a baby! We can't have a dog biting our baby!'

'That's a deal breaker,' said the husband, as the dog licked Joe's face, almost apologetically.

Suddenly Mum arrived, got a hold of Willow's collar and hauled her away from Joe. 'You naughty girl!' she said. Willow sat down and looked the picture of innocence, her tail thumping on the floor, as if she'd been a very good girl.

As he rubbed his bruised head, Joe felt a strange explosive sensation in his throat. He thought he might be about to have a coughing fit. But he actually had a laughing fit. Guffaws and giggles bubbled up out of him and he could do nothing to stop them.

The couple stared at him and then stalked away, slamming the gate behind them.

'Um… well, they really love it,' said the estate agent. 'They're considering an offer…'

'You think?' said Mum, leading Willow around to Mrs Ellis by her collar. 'Really?'

'They were just about to make an offer,' sighed the estate agent. 'If only that stupid dog hadn't ruined it all.'

'She's not stupid,' said Joe, surprising himself. 'But she's DANGEROUS,' he yelled after the departing house viewers. 'Very DANGEROUS!'

# Chapter 6

## Bert, Loki, Zing & Kizzi

I was in trouble for killing the bad sign but now it's a new day and they love me again.

We're going to the high park. I know this because we've gone the good way along the road and Jed has brought the whistle and the SPECIAL CHEWY CHICKEN STICK. The SPECIAL CHEWY CHICKEN STICK is tucked deep into his pocket but I can smell it. I might get it. I might not. It depends.

Down through the woods, over the river bridge and up the gravelly hill we go. Jed lets me pull on the lead when we go up the hill. It's the only time he lets me. At the top we stop and we look and Jed says: 'Who's here, then?'

Sometimes there's nobody. Sometimes there are only dogs on strings and they're no good. Dogs on strings have people on the end of the strings and these people don't seem to want my love. Sometimes they shout; especially when I get wrapped up in the string with their dog. Some of the dogs on strings say 'don't bother' and some of them say 'I wish I could but I'm on a string' and that's worse. That's just sad.

Today though, there are no dogs on strings. Today it's the Best Dogs. It's Loki and Zing and Bert. These are my friends. Loki is black and big like me and he can run as fast as me. Zing has long grey and white hair which floats as he runs. He can keep up with me and Loki. Bert is small and grey and furry with a grumpy bark. He runs like a table. He shouts at me whenever we meet. He shouts, 'Don't you think I'm taking any nonsense from you!' but then, after that, he decides to like me.

Kizzy is one of the best dogs too, but she's not here today. She is black and smaller than Bert and she dances on her back legs for treats. Kizzy is a new dog and she owns a lady. Zing is new too and he owns a lady, a man and a girl. Kizzy and Zing didn't come back for anyone.

Bert and Loki came back, though – like me. Bert owns two men, but he also half owns an older lady. Loki came back for the man and the woman he owns. Sometimes they call him Odin by mistake which is kind of funny, because he's not Odin any more. Bert has been called Jack once or twice. But their humans don't know. Some of them suspect, that's all.

We run and run and roll and wrestle and our people shout and call and laugh and talk to each other and collect poo. Loki tries to eat poo and everyone shouts. Loki doesn't care. 'There's good stuff still in that poo,' he tells us. Well…it's partly good, but most of it is bad and it makes him sick but he still goes back for more. I only like horse poo. And I only get that when we go to the big woods. When Jed isn't looking.

Our people talk to each other like we talk to each other. Today they are walking close together and the feel curls coming off them are… knotted up. They are worried. I hear them say 'Kizzy'. Maybe Kizzy is ill. Maybe she's had to go to the (whisper it, Granny always says) vet. I went to the vet and I was allowed up on a table. Scott lives at the vet and I like him. He gives me biscuits. He also makes me sleepy and once I was so sleepy I didn't wake up for a day and then my belly was sore for a week and I had to wear a round thing to stop me licking it better.

Has Kizzy gone to the vet? Has she gone to sleep and woken up wearing a round thing? Loki doesn't know and Bert doesn't think so. Zing thinks Kizzy ran away. But I don't think that because Kizzy isn't a running away type of dog. And anyway OH! OH! OH YEEEEESSS! I've found a story from a fox!

The wild dogs leave us such exciting stories. I smell the story in the grass and fall onto it before Loki can. I roll in the story and get all of it. It's a story of running and hunting and moonlight and digging. It's the best story ever. I can't get enough of it. I collect it all over my back and my neck and the top of my head so I can take it home and – 'Willow' – it has rabbits in it and squirrels and – 'WILLOW' – the wild dog is CATCHING the rabbit and – 'WILLOW! COME AWAY!' – the rabbit is warm and it's stopped being a rabbit and now it's food – 'WILLOW! STOP IT! COME HERE!'

Ah. The stories often end this way. Jed grabs my collar and hauls me off the story. Loki immediately gets onto it but his human starts yelling too and he's hauled away even quicker.

We almost NEVER get to the end of a fox story. It is a great unfairness. The foxes are something we need to know about. We long to know about them. I met one. He was wild. He was wonderful. I was running through the valley, ahead of Jed, and the fox stepped out and looked at me. I ran to love him and he just stood and looked and me until I stopped and sat down and my paw shook. And then he told me, 'No. No, dog. I am not for you.' And he smelt of the best fox story I have ever rolled in and I wanted to go with him.

But he said: 'No. No, dog. My life is not for you.'

I nearly cried actual tears, like I used to before, but the fox waved his tail at me as he vanished into the bushes and that was good. The tail said the fox liked me, even though I am a dog.

We don't meet any foxes on the way home, and Jed tells me off. He's going to have to hose me down in the garden. This is another good thing about the fox stories. I get the hose too and I like the hose. I like to bite the water rope. But then a man walks around the corner and Jed stops. He wedges me between his legs to stop me jumping up. But he doesn't need to.

'Lovely dog,' the man says. He has long floppy brown hair and small eyes. There is purple on his hand. A bit of rolled-up paper is stuck in his lips. Smoke is coming off it.

'Yeah, she's great,' says Jed, patting my head. 'A bit of a handful, though.'

The man leans down to me and the smoky paper makes my nose sting. There are other smells that are worse, though. This man has desperate, unhappy smells all over his hands and his clothes. He pats me on the head with his purple hand and I pull back from him and warn him to stop.

'Willow?' says Jed. 'What's with the growling? She's actually really friendly,' he says to the man.

25

'She's a beauty,' the man says, his small eyes shiny. 'I'd give you five hundred for her, cash.'

Jed steps back and I step back with him. 'She's not for sale,' says Jed and I think maybe he can smell the man's hands and clothes too, now, because there's no hello in his voice any more.

'Of course not,' says the man, standing up and smiling. 'Lovely thing like that – part of the family. I promised my little girl a doggie just like this. I wish I could afford one. My little girl's sick, you see.'

'I'm sorry to hear that,' says Jed.

'Maybe she can say hello to this doggie one day, if she's strong enough to walk down the road,' says the man. 'Which house are you?'

'We don't live around here,' says Jed. 'Sorry. Bye.' And he turns and walks us away from our house. Right to the end of the road and round the corner. We wait a little while and then go back again and into our house. The man has gone.

His feel curls are still in the air though. I shiver. It's not the first time I have seen the purple handed man. I remember the second thing I need to tell Joe. I need to tell him soon.

# Chapter 7

## Dog on a Hot Tin Roof

'How on earth did she get up there?'

Mum was staring out through the patio doors and gaping. Joe had only just got home and dropped his school bag in the hall when he heard her calling for him to come and see.

Willow was on top of their shed. Her front legs were splayed out flat, at a ninety degree angle, while her back end was high in the air and her eyes were riveted on Enid Blyton.

Enid Blyton was walking along the wall, looking as if she owned the whole street.

'Enid!' yelled Mum. 'Enid Blyton, you get off that wall immediately! Leave poor Willow alone!'

Joe realised their cat must have chased the dog right up on to the tin roof of the old shed. There were a few planks of wood stacked up against it and some crates, waiting to be filled with shed stuff as Mum sorted things out for the move. The dog must have somehow run up the crates and planks and then scrambled onto the roof.

'There's a lot of poodle in her,' said Mum. 'They're a very agile, bouncy breed. Willow! You need to get down!'

But no cat could yowl as scarily as Enid Blyton. The dog's tail gave an occasional pathetic wave, but then clamped right back again against its anxious back end. Mum strode through the garden and made a grab for Enid. For a cat named after a respected children's author, Enid Blyton was not at all well behaved. Most of the canines in their road had ended up with a bleeding nose after getting too close to the big tabby.

Mum managed to get hold of Enid. She clamped the hissing cat against her chest, taking her back into the house. 'See if you can get Willow down,' she called to Joe. 'And then take her back next door.'

Joe walked across the lawn, staring at the dog. 'You shouldn't even be in this garden,' he said. 'What do you think you're doing?!'

The dog bounced up on all four legs, her tail wagging furiously, making the tin roof rattle musically. Now that Enid Blyton had gone, it seemed delighted to be here.

'You've got to get down!' called Joe.

And the dog did get down. Right on top of him. Twenty-five kilos of furry fun suddenly knocked him flat onto his back in the grass.

'Doof!' said Joe. That was all. There was no breath left in him for more. He thought he might just have been crushed to death.

The dog sprung to its feet and starting licking his face, panting and making little growly sounds of delight. 'Gettoff! Gettoff!' spluttered Joe, finding some puff at last. He shoved the dog away and sat up, feeling a bit sick. Could you break your bum? It felt like he had.

'Are you trying to kill me or something?' muttered Joe. The dog sat down and tilted its head. It was quite a nice looking dog, he had to admit, especially when it wasn't right in his face.

'Look, you've got to go home,' he said, getting up and carefully rubbing the seat of his trousers. 'You shouldn't be here. Come on.'

He walked away and the dog trotted next to him, quite obediently.

Joe stopped for a moment, just as they reached the side passage. A droop had got him. Droops could land on him quite suddenly. At any time. One minute he was OK, then – wallop – a droop hit him and he felt like he and the whole world had dropped into a grey puddle. He pressed his hand against the old red brick of the house, and took a long breath. Willow stopped too. She put her nose into the curve of his other hand and breathed a warm breath into his palm. She seemed very still. As still as Joe was.

He looked down and saw two round black eyes fixed on him. The dog did that head tilt again, as if she was saying: 'What's up, kid?' He felt a sad smile crease his face and patted the dog's head. 'Just… stuff,' he said. 'I don't want to move away. And… ah never mind.'

He walked on down the passage and Willow followed. Then Mum opened the side door and Willow did an abrupt right turn and crashed into the house.

# Chapter 8

## Emily's Room

At last! Finally I get a chance. The side door opens a crack and I flow through it like water, pushing it aside, speedily nudging my head past two legs and slipping slightly on the tiled floor. The kitchen smells good as I scrabble for grip. There's cheese on the worktop and I love cheese – but this is not about cheese. This is about the room. I knew, as soon as Jed brought me to my new home and I realised where we were, that I must get back to the room.

I hurl myself along the polished wooden floorboards of the hallway and do what Jed calls my 'handbrake turn' at the foot of the stairs. There is carpet on the steps, which is good. I can get a proper grip as I race up to the landing. Behind me there are shouts of alarm and I know I am being a Bad Dog but that's not important right now. It might be later, but not now. Now I have to get upstairs. I have to get to the room. I have to!

'Willow, come back here!'

Suddenly Joe is grabbing me around the waist and pushing me down onto the landing floor. 'What are you doing?!' he asks. I twist around in his grip, rolling onto the carpet and flipping over to show off my belly. My front paws do what Jed calls 'the rabbit thing'; they are lifted up to my chest and flapping up and down. The back paws waggle in the air. I roll my eyes and put out my tongue, panting. This is the PLAY WITH ME pose I use for humans. Usually they laugh and start rubbing my belly or playing with my flappy paws.

Joe is no exception. I hear him laugh for the first time in forever as he starts to play. 'You're so naughty,' he says, lifting first one front paw and letting it drop and then the other.

I wag my tail hard, pummelling the floor with it, and make my best growly conversation. Joe's hair is floppier than I remember but he smells mostly the same. I try to lick his face; get a proper taste so I can know more – but he splutters and pushes me away.

'Come on,' he says, reaching for my collar. 'It's time you went home, you bad dog.'

I leap up and bounce out of his reach. I bounce towards the bathroom. It's full of Joe smells; they swim up out of a basket, which is full of the clothes he's worn. It's always a great sadness to my kind when these lovely smells are taken away by a noisy machine in the kitchen. All these clothes which have been filled with wonderful odours until they are perfectly beautiful… they go into the machine and it attacks them with water and soap until they are empty again. A washing machine is an unhappy thing.

But I don't go into the bathroom. As Joe tries to grab me again I duck down and jump sideways until I'm just outside the room. I boop the door with my nose but it's fast shut, so

I leap up against it, my claws clicking and sliding on the white shiny surface. It shakes but it doesn't open. I lick it.

'NO!' thunders Joe. But I jump up again, catch the handle of the door, and fall into the room.

Everything goes quiet.

The room smells just the same. It's tidier than I remember but the bed is the same colour – green. The walls are green too, with flat leaves growing up and down, which do not move or smell.

The buggy is just exactly the same. I could jump up into it and sit down and feel it under me… but I do not. I do not need the buggy now. Nobody needs to wheel me around. I can run and bounce and leap and walk and it is the BEST thing.

I don't remember everything. I don't think you can remember everything – it would make you fall on the floor; the weight of all that memory. Bert says he remembers things in little chunks. He says he's sure he remembered big chunks when he was new, but the chunks have got smaller as he's got bigger. His life now takes up more space than his life then. But he remembers the important thing – the love.

The room has boxes in one corner and I see things in the boxes that I remember. Clothes – white and yellow and green and pink. The washing machine has attacked them so they don't smell like before. There are books too. And a machine with buttons and tubes and a wire that went round my old head.

And there is a picture of Joe and Mum… and old me. Our faces are all squashed together in a rectangle and we are laughing and one of my eyes is closed. I turn to see real Joe.

He does not look like picture Joe. He is not laughing. 'You shouldn't be in here!' he yelps. 'This is Emily's room.'

I sit still and look at him. And then I do the only thing I can think of. I nod three times.

# Chapter 9

# Nodding Dog

Joe stood in Emily's room and stared at the dog. This was so WRONG.

'You shouldn't be in here – this is EMILY'S room!' he yelled, a sob catching in his throat. He hadn't been in here for over a year. He couldn't believe it looked just the same.

He glared at the dog. It was suddenly quiet and sitting still and then… to his amazement… it nodded its head. Three times. Very definitely. Joe sank down on to the bed, gaping.

'Are you alright up there?' Mum called up the stairs.

'Um… yeah…' Joe called back, in a weird, high voice. 'We'll be down in a minute.'

He stared at the dog for a few seconds and it stared back at him. 'You just… you just nodded…' he muttered.

The dog nodded again. Joe nearly fell off the bed.

'You nodded three times!' he gasped.

The dog nodded once more… three times.

Joe rubbed his hands over his face. He must be imagining this. 'Am I imagining this?' he breathed.

The dog tilted its head for a moment and then… very definitely… shook its head. Left to right. Three times.

'That's just… exactly… what Emily used to do!' murmured Joe, feeling goosebumps rush all over his skin.

The dog nodded three times.

Joe closed his eyes and took a long, slow breath. 'But Emily died over a year ago.' It still made him crunch up inside to say the words aloud. Emily had been two years older than him, but much smaller. She had been in a wheelchair for all the time he'd known her. She could make noises but she couldn't really speak. She would nod and shake her head… and because she couldn't help sometimes twitching or shaking, she had to be very clear about the actions she intended to make. She would always nod or shake her head three times.

How could this dog possibly know about this? How could it sit here and mimic the dead girl who used to live here?

An answer kept trying to snake its way into his head. A stupid, ridiculous, crazy answer.

He opened his eyes and saw the dog had shuffled closer to him and was fixing him with an intense stare; its tail thumping on the floor.

Joe got up and closed the door. He leant against it and said: 'Willow… are you my sister? Are you Emily? Have you… come back as a dog?'

The dog nodded three times.

# Chapter 10

## Seriously? Emily?

Joe's face goes very pink. He keeps shaking his head. Then he gets to his feet and grabs the picture off the wall. He points to Mum and says: 'OK... is this you?'

I stare at the picture and then up at him for a second. Of course that's not me! I shake my head. He gulps. His feel curls are spinning around me like leaves in a storm and they smell of everything. They are excited, and sad, and happy, and angry and confused and scared and amazed…

'So… is this you?' he points to himself. I sigh loudly and shake my head.

His finger shakes as he points to his sister. Me. When I was here before. I nod my head three times. He sinks to his knees, dropping the picture onto the carpet, and puts his face close to mine.

'Seriously? Emily? You've come back as a dog?'

I nod and lick his nose. So stop feeling so sad, little brother. I wish I had words. Dogs have many more skills than humans, of course. We hear better, smell better, taste better, run better… but we can't make words and that, for a dog like me, can be annoying. Because humans don't have the power to understand very much if it isn't in words.

'Have I got a granddad called Ted?' he asks, suddenly.

Not as far as I know. I suppose he could have got a granddad called Ted while I was away… but I don't think so. I shake my head.

'Have I got an aunty called Joanne?'

I nod and then I go and get a book that's lying on the desk by the window – a book about dogs, as it happens. I can't read but I remember the pictures. It was one of my favourites. Aunty Jo gave it to me.

I take the book in my teeth and dump it in Joe's lap and he suddenly puts his arms around me and squeezes me tight. 'It's OK,' he says. 'I believe you now. I believe you've come back as a dog. You always said you would.'

Over on the buggy is a flat, square thing that I used to use to make words. I remember it from when I had hands. They were difficult hands to use but I could press the buttons and make words.

And yes… I always did want to come back as a dog one day. I am pleased Joe remembers.

I want to remind him of other things but there is suddenly a bell ringing and then a voice calls up: 'Joe! It's Mrs Ellis. Please bring Willow down.'

And so we walk downstairs, where Granny tells me off for jumping over the fence, but I am not sad because Joe says: 'Can I take her out for a walk? Tomorrow, maybe?'

And Granny smiles and says yes. I leap up to kiss her and she bats me down. 'Willow! DOWN!'

It's hard to stay down. I have told Joe the first thing! He KNOWS! I look quickly at the colour of the wall by our gate and promise myself that tomorrow – somehow – I will tell him the second thing.

# Chapter 11

## Temporary Sister

Almost as soon as he'd left Willow… or Emily… and gone back to his house, Joe began to doubt himself.

It couldn't be real. It couldn't. Could it…?

Emily had died just over a year ago. Joe had always known she wasn't going to live long. Mum had explained to him as far back as he could remember, that Emily was different. She had an illness which meant she couldn't walk or talk and she would never grow up. She was… temporary.

It was still a horrible shock when Emily did exactly what Mum had told him she would one day do. She'd died. Mum had been expecting it but Joe hadn't. Although he had known… he hadn't really known. He hadn't even been there when Emily had died; he'd been out. He'd felt so bad about not saying goodbye that he had never gone into her room again. He just couldn't bear to see it empty.

But today – when he finally had gone in – Emily had been there after all. Only she was four-legged and covered in woolly black dog hair and wagging a tail about.

He must be imagining it. This kind of thing wasn't real.

No. He was just… making it up to make himself feel better. That was it. He would take Willow out tomorrow to the park and when he asked her questions this time, she wouldn't be able to answer. She had just been randomly nodding and shaking her head today. She probably had an ear infection or something.

'Too bad about the house viewers,' Mum said, as he wandered into the kitchen. 'Willow put them right off.' She sighed.

'Good,' said Joe. 'They were horrible. They wanted to gut the bathroom and pull out the fireplace… and they laughed at your curtains.'

Mum sighed. 'I know this is hard, Joe,' she said. 'I wish we didn't have to move, too. But it's been so hard getting back into full-time work since… since Emily went… and I'm just not earning enough to pay for this place.'

Joe nodded, staring at his feet. He didn't want to make things worse for Mum. He knew she'd tried hard to keep the house. When Emily had got really ill Mum had left her job to look after her – and then, after Emily died, when Mum had felt ready to go back to work, she just couldn't find anything that paid as well. She could only get part time work at a local shop and the pay wasn't great.

'When the house is sold we might even have a bit of money for a holiday,' Mum said, trying to sound cheerful.

Mum had done a lot of trying to sound cheerful for the past year.

Joe sank onto the chair at the table. He decided he did NOT believe his sister had come back as Willow, the dog who lived next door. Because if he had to leave this house and move away he would lose Emily all over again. And he could not bear that.

'It's OK, Mum,' he said. 'We'll be alright. It might even be better, living on the other side of town.'

Outside, he distinctly heard a howl.

# Chapter 12

## The Purple on the Wall

Smoky Lip Man walks past the garden as I wait. I get his feel curls way before he arrives, so I am hiding under the hedge as he walks past. He smells as bad as ever and I know Joe and I have to do something about it. I can't decide whether Thing 2 or Thing 3 is more important.

A new bad sign is back up again. It creaks when the wind blows. I can't read it but I know it's telling people to come to the house; to push Joe and Mum out and push themselves in. No wonder Joe is angry. I am angry. If I lived there still I wouldn't let any of those people as far as the door.

A short while after Smoky Lip Man has gone Joe arrives at the gate. I leap up to love him and he pushes me down and says: 'NO!' His feel curls are tangled and confused so I sit down and wait for him to sort himself out.

He gets the lead from Granny and we set out on a walk. At the gate I stop and sniff the purple on the wall and growl at it, but Joe doesn't notice and just tugs me away, off down the road. He thinks we're going to the park but we're not. We have to go somewhere else.

'Stop pulling!' puffs Joe, as I drag him along the pavement. 'Why can't you behave?!'

I keep pulling until he hisses: 'Look! If you really are Emily – STOP!'

Gah! He's got me. I have to stop. I turn to look at him and I sit down. He leans against a garden wall and stares at me while his feel curls leap around him. Of course I'm Emily. I wish I could say it in words but all I can do is give him the look. Also, I am Willow too, now. I like my new name.

'I thought I was imagining it,' says Joe, shaking his head. 'Just... to be sure. If you're really Emily, nod at me again.'

I nod three times.

'If you're really Emily, turn around on the spot.'

I turn around on the spot.

'If you're really Aunty Jane, turn around on the spot again.'

Oh-ho. A trick. I sigh and tilt my head, standing still. This is getting quite tiring.

'OK,' says Joe. He keeps staring at me. We really don't have time for this. I will lose the scent soon and that will mess up Thing 2. Thing 2 is very serious. Joe needs to know. I stand up and flip my head in the direction we need to go.

'Are you taking me somewhere?' asks Joe. 'Only... I thought I was taking you somewhere.'

I sigh again and flip my head again.

'OK, OK – lead the way!' he says – at last. And so I turn and walk as fast as I can, until he's running behind me and laughing. It's been such a long time since he has laughed that it fills me with leaps and bounds of joy.

But when I think about where we are going, the leaps and bounds get smaller and then they hide away inside me. Where we are going, everything hides away inside everyone.

# Chapter 13

# A Whimper in the Dark

They weren't going anywhere near the park. Emily/Willow led him along several roads, through the High Street and round the corner past the post office and along the stretch of boardwalk by the river. This was the prettiest part of their town and there was a row of cafes, gift shops and other entertainments for visitors and locals. As they reached the Gold Rush Arcade, the dog paused, looked round at him, and then stared intently inside.

Joe felt goosebumps as he slowed to a halt. 'Do you... do you remember this place?' he asked. His sister nodded and looked up at him, her mouth wide open and her tongue lolling out sideways – as if she was laughing.

'Yeah,' said Joe. 'We had fun in there, didn't we?' The labradoodle nodded three times.

Joe could hear the jingling and chiming of electronic music from the machines. The Gold Rush was a touristy place with some old-fashioned video games, some fruit machines (with a jackpot of silver coins, not strawberries) and one of those grab-a-toy crane things which never picked anything up no matter how many goes you had. There was also a big hexagonal machine called the Penny Falls.

This is what Emily had loved the most. Every so often on a summer weekend Mum would take them along the boardwalk by the river and they would go into The Gold Rush. Joe loved playing the retro games like Space Invaders and Pac Man on the big old consoles – and Emily loved to watch him. Then they would play the Penny Falls. They didn't have much money, but Mum could spare a small amount for each for them. Sitting in her buggy, her hands curled up against her shoulders, Emily would laugh and laugh as Joe put her pennies in for her. She could make a chortling noise every time she wanted him to let a coin drop. Then she'd watch, fascinated, as the coin fell down in a zig-zag between the pins and settled on one of the ever-moving shelves, ready to shove the other coins along and over the edge.

Of course, even when they'd created some spectacular avalanches, they would always keep feeding their winnings back in until they'd lost all their money again. Mum would laugh when it was all gone and say nobody wanted to carry around that much copper anyway. And sometimes, before they left, she would buy each of them a £1 scratch card. None of them would scratch it straight away – oh no. That wasn't the game at all. They had to keep their cards in their pockets all the way home and talk about what they would buy with their winnings if they scratched away the silvery stuff to reveal the big prize - £100,000.

Of course, they never won anything more than £10 – but that wasn't the point. It was the daydreaming that was the point. Joe wanted a Ferrari racing car, a trampoline, a tree house, a massive flat screen TV, a holiday to Australia... Mum said she'd get the house fixed up a bit and take them all to watch the Northern Lights in Iceland... Emily didn't say much, of course, but sometimes she would make her fingers work on her little portable keyboard and she had nearly always written the same thing.

DOG.

Joe blinked away tears as he watched her now, staring at the Penny Falls and being the thing she had wanted most in the world.

'You loved the Penny Falls the best, didn't you, Emily?' he said and the dog nodded, still staring dreamily into the arcade. 'Look,' he said, suddenly aware of people passing nearby, 'if I keep calling you Emily someone's going to hear... someone who knows about... you... before.'

The dog looked up at him and gave a short upward twitch of her furry chin. 'And they're going to think I've gone mad.' She nodded. 'So... are you OK if I call you Willow when we're out and about?'

She nodded and wagged her tail enthusiastically. 'Do you like the name Willow?' She nodded again. 'Fine then... Willow it is,' he said. 'Except sometimes.' He was just about to see if he could sneak her into the arcade when she suddenly started moving on down the pavement again, pulling hard against the lead.

'Hey – slow down, Willow!' he called. 'Where are you off to now?'

But Willow didn't slow down. She kept pulling him along until he started to run with her. He had no idea why but she seemed to be very certain where she was going. After ten minutes they were some distance from the river in a narrow, grimy backstreet with a row of terraced houses on one side and a sprawling grey car repair centre on the other. The whole place smelt of diesel and engine oil. A mud spattered street sign read: Aker Close.

'What are we doing here?' grumbled Joe. 'We should go back.'

But Willow trotted on to the far end of the fence around the car repair centre. Almost hidden from view, by a huge straggly buddleia bush and a rusty white van parked across the pavement, was an old bungalow. Its garden was so overgrown you could hardly see the peeling front door. The grass was beaten down to one side in a sort of path, though, and the rusty wrought iron front gate hung open on one hinge. Willow stopped by the gate, sniffed the air, and gave a low growl.

'What is it?' whispered Joe, suddenly feeling goosebumps across his shoulders. He did not want to walk up that path, but it looked like they were going to. Willow nosed the gate until it opened with a metallic groan. Once inside she turned and gave Joe a hard stare before flipping her snout towards the bungalow.

'This is where you wanted to go?' he asked, puzzled and a little scared. 'Why? Is there a person here you want me to meet?'

Her eyes rolled and she shook her head three times.

'OK – you don't want me to meet the person who lives here?'

She nodded three times. Correct.

'So why are we here?' he whispered, glancing around to see if they were being watched. There didn't seem to be anyone around.

Suddenly Willow was off again, pulling him right past the front door and along a side passage towards a tall gate made of damp, stained chipboard. They reached the gate. Stuck to it was a piece of paper in a plastic sleeve. Scrawled on the paper in red felt tip was the message: Granby Woods. 11. 21. Willow jumped up at it, thudding her paws and claws against it loudly.

'Shhhh!' Joe looked around anxiously. The whole sideway stunk like a toilet which hadn't been cleaned for a year. 'Why do you want to go in here?'

In reply, she just whimpered.

'Oh, alright,' grunted Joe, shaking his head but reaching up and undoing the loop of thick string holding the gate shut. He pulled the gate open and Willow flowed through the widening gap in a determined current of fur.

The passageway was even darker and damper. Joe shivered. He really did not want to be here. Willow didn't look too keen, either. Her tail was flat against the back of her legs and that low growl was still rumbling away inside her.

'We shouldn't be here!' whispered Joe, tugging on her lead. Then he heard something. It sounded like a whimper… but it wasn't coming from Willow. Willow's head snapped around; she had heard it too. There was a mildew-spotted window in the wall just above Joe's left shoulder. It probably led into a toilet or cupboard. It was slightly ajar. Joe put up a shaking hand and pulled it a little wider open.

A sour smell wafted out of it. And another whimper. Willow suddenly leapt up at the window, letting out a sharp bark.

'Shhhh! Shhhh!' Joe grabbed her woolly shoulders and hauled her away. But too late – there was a shout from inside the bungalow.

'Oi!' came a harsh voice. 'Cut that out!'

There was another whimper and then Willow went off again, lunging back towards the window and letting out a wild volley of angry barks.

'WHO'S THAT?!' yelled the voice and Joe dragged Willow back down the side passage, thumping past the damp hardboard gate and out into the weedy front garden. His heart was pounding and it was all he could do to keep hold of the lead; Willow was pulling so hard against him.

'Come ON!' he hissed, tearing past the wonky metal front gate. 'Willow! Willow! EMILY!'

At last his sister seemed to snap out of her wild fit of barking and realised he NEEDED her to RUN. And not a moment too soon because the side gate crashed open and a thin, unshaven man in a stained jumper and jeans stomped out towards them.

'Whatchodoininmyyard?!' he bellowed, wiping his long lanky hair off his face.

'Sorry,' yelled back Joe, over his shoulder. 'She ran off… I just came to get her back. Sorry…'

The man shouted something else unrepeatable and then went back inside. Willow finally began to walk normally again, back the way they'd come, her head down and her tail low.

'What was all that about?' asked Joe. 'Why did you do that?' He remembered the whimpering and felt a deep unease. Once they were safely around the corner he knelt down and looked directly into Willow's eyes. 'Were you... I mean... do you know who was whimpering in there?'

She gave a little, sad nod.

'Are they in trouble?' he asked.

Another nod.

Joe stood up again, thinking hard, and said: 'I can't just go in there and ask to see whoever it was who was whimpering.' Willow didn't look up at him but just kept her head and her tail down as they headed for home. 'I don't really know what I can do,' he added. Willow didn't respond. He felt bad – and then annoyed. He was only just getting over the shock and amazement of finding out his sister was reincarnated as a labradoodle. He was shaken up enough as it was without now having to worry about some mysterious whimpering in a stinky bungalow.

'Look... I'll have a think,' he said, walking on. 'Maybe talk to Mum.' That was going to be tricky though. How on earth could he explain why he and next door's dog had suddenly gone on a little tour of the roughest part of town?

He tried to stop thinking about it – he had enough to get his head around! But for some reason that odd red ink sign kept floating back through his head:

Granby Woods. 11. 21.

What did that mean?

# Chapter 14

## No Kizzy

I had almost forgotten about Thing 3 but I'm reminded of it when we get home and Joe takes me back to Granny and Jed. 'Thank you, Joe!' 'says Granny at the door. 'Did you go to the park?'

'Um. No – we just went along the river and back,' says Joe. He doesn't talk about the Dark Place. I want him to talk about the Dark Place and I stare up at him and paw at his leg. He drops down to my level and looks into my eyes. 'We'll go out again tomorrow, OK, Em-Willow.' He goes a bit pink because he nearly called me Emily again, so I lick his nose to tell him I understand. He is going to have a think and we will do something about the Dark Place tomorrow.

I don't mind him calling me Emily. I'm happy to be Willow, though. As Emily I could never walk or run or lick people's faces or talk. As Willow I still can't talk, but I can do all the other things. Better than a human, too!

'She does love going out with you!' says Granny. 'She'll miss you when you move away.'

Joe stands up and sighs, glancing across at the For Sale sign. 'I'll miss her too,' he says.

'It's a shame,' says Granny, giving my head a rub as he walks back next door. 'They've had such a rotten run of luck.'

I eat my dinner and have a little sleep. I dream of biting Smoky Lip Man. Hard. Then he turns into a rabbit. Then the rabbit turns into food but I don't eat it. It smells bad.

'Oi – furryface!' says a voice, and Jed is there with my lead. 'Stop growling in your sleep! Come on – it's time for a quick run around the park before tea.'

At the park Bert, Loki and Zing run over for a chase. For a while I chase with them. Loki has a crackly bottle in his teeth and we all try to get it. When I get it I run fast with my chase me flag up at the back. The bottle tastes sweet and orangey. Zing gets it off me and it's only when Zing stops to do a poo that everyone slows down. Which is quite right. You don't play chase me when a friend is doing a poo.

Loki sniffs at it and declares Zing fit and well. Then he gets pulled away by his human before he can eat it. Bert stands for a moment. Then he looks at me and says, 'No Kizzy'.

I look around the park. Bert is right. There is still no Kizzy.

I had hoped I was wrong.

# Chapter 15

## 11.21

Joe's heart sank as he went indoors and heard voices. It was another viewing.

Someone was in the front room with the estate agent. He could tell this with his nostrils; the estate agent wore so much aftershave you could smell him even before he got out of his car. It was like being punched in the nose.

'We'd have to have the carpet up,' a woman was saying. 'I hope the floorboards are good.'

'If they are, that ticks a box,' a man said.

Joe was tempted to pop his head around the door and inform them that there was nothing but concrete under the carpet. And it was really damp. But he'd be lying – there were some really nice floorboards; Mum had talked about taking up the old carpet and getting the boards varnished a while ago, but they couldn't afford to do it.

He spotted Mum waving to him from the garden, so he walked on through the kitchen and out through the open back door. He was surprised to find that Mum wasn't alone.

'Hi Joe,' said Ben. 'I cycled here today so you're in less danger. Probably.'

'Oh,' said Joe. 'I wondered whose bike was chained up out the front.'

'I bumped into your mum on the way home,' said Ben. 'Wait – let me say that again. I happened to meet your mum on the way home. No bumping occurred.'

'Cup of tea and a chat time,' said Mum, holding up a steaming mug. 'Just to keep my mind off that lot.' She rolled her eyes towards the house and then whispered: 'The woman isn't sure about the shape of the windows. I don't know what shape she wants. Round? Hexagonal shaped? Star shaped?'

'Spongebob Squarepants shaped?' added Joe.

They all laughed. 'Maybe they don't want it,' said Joe. 'Maybe they only came round so they can decide whether to come back and burgle us later. We should set Enid Blyton on them.'

Mum snorted into her tea but Ben shook his head. 'Don't say that! It happens, you know.'

'Well, you ought to know,' said Mum. Then she looked at Joe and gestured towards Ben. 'He's a policeman, remember,' she said, in a dramatic whisper.

Ben laughed. 'Well, when I'm not busy trying to mow down children,' he said.

Just then the house viewers came into the garden, so they all hurried down to the end to get out of the way. But not before they heard the woman say: 'This garden definitely needs some decking.' She seemed to be fixated on planks.

'I don't suppose you get to arrest many people around here,' said Mum, as they loitered behind the greenhouse.

'You'd be surprised,' said Ben. 'A lot of crime goes on, even in a nice place like this.'

Joe had a sudden thought, out of nowhere. 'Ben,' he said. 'Does anything criminal go on up at Granby Woods?'

Ben shrugged: 'A fair bit, I suppose. People get drunk up there sometimes in the summer – and get into fights. Stolen cars get dumped there once in a while. We swing by from time to time, on a night shift. I've made a few arrests up there myself.'

Joe didn't say anything else because the estate agent was now trotting down the garden, waving at Mum. The couple had gone back in the house.

'They like it!' the estate agent said, looking rather pink. 'I think they're going to make an offer.'

'Excellent,' said Mum.

Joe glanced at Ben. Ben gave him a sympathetic look. It seemed he didn't want them to move either.

'Don't worry,' Ben said, as they walked back up the path. 'Your Mum knows what she's doing. I'm sure you'll get used to the flat really quickly. Uh-oh!' He checked his watch. 'I'd better get going. On duty at fourteen hundred hours!'

Joe went to his room once everyone had gone, leaving Mum downstairs, glumly watching TV. He kept turning over the day's events in his head; trying to make sense of them.

1. He had confirmed that his sister had come back as a dog.
2. HIS SISTER HAD COME BACK AS A DOG!
3. It was OK. He was actually very happy about Emily coming back as Willow.

4.    She'd taken him to a weird old bungalow and made him trespass down its sideway.

5.    Something had been whimpering inside the bungalow – and Willow was upset by it.

6.    They'd been chased away by a scary man.

7.    Willow expected him to do something about it.

And the other thing that kept going around his head was that sign.

Granby Woods. 11. 21.

What did it mean? Was it a meeting or something? 11. 21. That could be a date. But if so, it could only be the 21st of November – and this was August. He glanced at his watch. August 11, actually. Wait a minute! What if that's what it meant? The eleventh day of this month... today.

Then what did 21 mean? He suddenly heard Ben again, saying: 'On duty at fourteen hundred hours!' Well... 21 could mean twenty one hundred hours. Nine in the evening.

Joe sat up. If it was a meeting, it would be tonight. Tonight at nine in Granby Woods. Maybe the sign was up there for other people to read – people who knew the code. So... would that nasty long-haired guy be going out tonight? If so, there might not be anyone else around in that bungalow. It might be safe to go back there and sniff around with Willow; see if they could find whatever was whimpering; maybe rescue it!

Joe sighed and lay back down again. Come on! He told himself. You're not going to go running around with Willow late at night! That's stupid. Just... tell Ben! Yes. That was the thing to do. Tell Ben.

But… how could he get Ben's number? He could ask Mum but she would want to know why. Telling her that he and Willow wanted to rescue some mystery whimpering creature from a stranger's bungalow was going to throw up a whole load of other questions. Joe wracked his brains for any other believable reason why he might want to phone Ben. He couldn't think of a thing.

Downstairs the landline phone rang. Joe listened in as Mum took the call. 'Oh… that's great,' she said. 'Well… that's not a bad offer. OK. Well… let me think it over and call you back in the morning.'

He heard the click as she put down the phone. Then there was a small pause. Then she called up to him, softly: 'Joe… I think we've sold the house.'

# Chapter 16

## Bike Run

A most unexpected thing happens when I go out for my late night toilet stop in the garden.

I'm just finishing up when I get a whopping great feel curl coming over the fence. Joe is there! Just the other side. I have never smelt Joe in the garden at this hour. It's been dark for some time. He smells excited and a bit scared.

I run to the fence and bounce up on it with my front paws. 'Shhhhh!' he says, as I lick his nose. 'We've got to go... quietly! Can you get over here? Or shall I come around to your gate and let you out?'

Can I get over there?! Seriously?! I back up a bit and then clear the fence in one leap, landing softly on the grass.

'OK,' says Joe, in a quiet voice. 'Mum thinks I've gone to sleep, but I think we need to go back to that place. That place you took me today'

I nod. Three times.

'I think the man will be out... so we might be able to get in through that window... maybe. I don't know. In fact... I don't know why I'm doing this. I must be bonkers.' He smells as if he's changing his mind and that's not good. I really want to go back there. I really must go back there.

I sit down and do the ultimate thing. I gaze up at him and then… the head tilt. Almost nobody in the world can resist the head tilt.

'Oh, alright then,' he mutters, rubbing me behind the ears. 'I won't be able to sleep anyway, thinking about that poor whimpering creature, whatever it is. OK… you need to wait here a moment.'

I stay sitting, waiting in silence while he goes into the shed. A passing bat swoops down, wondering what I'm doing out and about at this hour. Joe comes back wheeling his bike. It makes a gentle brrrrrrr noise as he brings it closer. A plastic thing hangs off one handlebar. Joe unhooks it and looks at it. 'I don't like wearing a bike helmet,' he says. 'But I should probably try to be safe… and also it's got a peak at the front and that might hide my face a bit, in case we meet anyone on the road.'

He puts the hat on, clicking the strap under his chin, the way Jed clicks my strap on my collar, under my chin. Then he heads off down the side passage with the bike. 'Sssh,' he says. 'They're going to come out and call for you at any moment. You have to stay quiet if they do.'

But they don't come out and call. Sometimes I'm out in the garden for quite a long time while Jed and Granny are back in the house, staring at the TV. Sometimes they forget me. Sometimes I call out to be let in and then they're all guilty and give me biscuits and hugs because they forgot me. But sometimes, in the summer when it's warm and all the smells are floating, I like to stay in the garden. I hope they forget tonight because I don't know when we are coming back.

Out on the street, Joe puts a white light on at the front of his bike and a red light on at the back. 'Battery's a bit low on the back one,' he mutters. 'But it should be OK. Right… you're off the lead, Em-Willow… so you have to be responsible. You have to run along the pavement and stay close to me, OK?'

I nod and Joe takes a deep breath, glances back at the house, and then sets off along the road. He moves much faster than this afternoon, whizzing along on two wheels – but I love to run and I can keep up easily. We head along, side by side, Joe on the road and me on the pavement, towards the shops and the lights and the river. There are people around, walking in twos and threes, and some of them say: 'Ooooh – look at the dog!' as we run by. Normally I would leap at them with love but there is no time tonight so I keep on running.

When we reach The Gold Rush I can't help looking in and sniffing. It's all lit up and twinkly and quite a lot of people are inside, playing. But there is no time to stop and we keep on running.

As we get close, and the streets get darker and quieter, my insides are scrunched up but still jumping about. Can we help? Can we really help? I glance up at Joe, pedalling hard alongside me, and see the look on his face. Joe's feel curls are like mine – scrunched up and jumping about – but Joe is brave. Joe looks like he could do anything.

At last we reach the Dark Place. The road is very dark as Joe slows down on his bike and gets off it, wheeling it along. The place with lots of cars behind a fence is dim and gloomy.

I can see much better at night than I used to before, though, so I slow down and look around me, and get a good sniff of what's happening.

And what's happening is not good.

# Chapter 17

# A Whimper in the Dark

Joe began to feel stupid when they reached the road. As he slowed down on the bike he could feel his legs trembling – and it wasn't just because they were tired after all that pedalling. Willow slowed down too, as he stopped the bike, hopped off it and started wheeling it along. What was he doing here?! This was mad! He shouldn't be out on his own at night – he should be back home in bed!

But a lick on his hand reminded him he wasn't on his own. He had his sister with him… and his sister could run and jump and, if necessary, bite, like a superhero. At the corner of the road, Joe leant his bike against the Akers Close sign and switched off its lights. He should probably lock it, but… if they needed to get away fast, that would be a problem. In the end he decided to drape the lock around the crossbar and over the sign to make it look like it was locked.

Then he started walking, Willow close at his side. Neither of them spoke; Willow because she couldn't and Joe because he daren't. Willow's head was close to his side though and he could feel her breath on his palm. He knew she was as nervous as he was. As they reached the chain-link fence at the front of the car repair place, Joe took a deep breath. Would that long-haired man be gone? Off meeting someone in Granby Woods to get drunk or something? He checked his watch – it was 9.33pm – so the meeting had started half an hour ago. The house should be empty.

Of course, that sign might have meant something completely different; it could have been a map reference or… an order for takeaway food… or… anything! Joe held his breath as they reached the bungalow. It was in darkness. The van that had been parked across the kerb was nowhere to be seen. The gate was still hanging open.

Willow glanced up at him and led the way in. Across the road there were lights in the windows of the houses; people sitting down and watching TV, having their dinners, behaving like normal people. And here he was, sneaking around outside a smelly old bungalow well after his bedtime with his sister who was reincarnated as a dog.

The side passage smelt just as bad as he followed the dim woolly outline of Willow, padding quietly ahead of him. They reached the side gate and he unlooped the bit of string at the top and pushed it open to find more gloom and another wave of bad smell. He got out his torch and shone it along the damp passage. Behind them the gate swung closed with a loud creak, making him catch his breath and freeze, but after a few seconds he couldn't hear anyone coming outside to check on the noise.

And then he did hear something. It was high pitched… almost too high to hear… Willow heard it instantly. She leapt up against the wall beneath the high window, which was still ajar, and gave a low whine.

'Who is it?' Joe whispered, feeling chills racing up and down his spine.

Now he heard the whimpering again. Something was definitely in there and definitely very unhappy. Willow began to jump repeatedly against the window, knocking it wider open with her snout.

'Shhhhh!' hissed Joe. 'Wait! We need to think about this!' Willow dropped back and turned an anxious circle as he shone the torch up at the window. It opened at the level of his head; just a little too high for him to easily see inside. Could he fit through? It would be tight but he thought he could. He just needed to find a way to get up there.

'Come on,' he whispered. 'We need to find a ladder or something.' He followed his torch beam on down the passage and around the corner of the bungalow.

The back garden was even more overgrown than the front – the weeds were up to his waist. There was a shed but when he tried the door he found it was secured with a rusty padlock. Ah – but there was something up against one side of it; a kind of trolley with a heavy canister in it. It was one of those gas-powered barbecues.

Joe snorted with nervous laughter, trying to imagine anyone ever having a barbecue in a garden like this; people standing around in t-shirts and shorts, in the waist high weeds, chatting to each other over hot dogs and beef burgers, ignoring the stench and the occasional rat running over their feet while they drank bubbly wine.

There was a flat-topped metal lid on the barbecue. Joe lifted it and shone his torch on the metal grill beneath. A single blackened sausage lay there, looking like the finger of a recently discovered Egyptian mummy. Joe snorted with nervous laughter again.

OK. Concentrate. He found a metal rung on the back of the barbecue and pulled on it. The wheels made a gritty noise and then they started to turn. Willow followed closely as Joe wheeled the heavy trolley around into the side passage with a dull rumble and pushed it up against the wall, just beneath the window.

'OK,' he said. "I think I can – GAH!'

Willow had lost no time. She'd worked out exactly what it was for and had leapt up onto it and bounded through the open window within two seconds. Joe gasped as he saw her back paws vanish through the gap and then heard her land, with a click and scrape of her claws, on the floor beyond.

'Willow! You should have waited!' he muttered, clambering up onto the barbecue. He poked his head through the window, shining the torch, and saw that it was a cupboard... an old-style pantry with shelves filled with boxes and bottles. The cupboard door stood open and Willow was nowhere to be seen.

Joe held on to the top of the window frame and put his legs over the ledge. It was very tight and awkward. Happily there was a big box just below the sill on the inside and he was able to wriggle through and get his feet down onto it, using it as a step.

Once on the sticky vinyl floor, Joe took a breath and then held it. He was in a small, under-stairs cupboard, filled with boxes and sacks. The smell was really bad. He covered his nose and mouth with one hand and directed the torch beam with the other, following Willow out past an open door into the hallway. 'Willow!' he whispered. 'Where are you?' He heard her give a low wuff in reply and followed the sound to the front of the bungalow, past the small hallway and front door to his left, and on into the main sitting room.

It wasn't a sitting room you'd ever want to sit in. For a start, there was nothing to sit on. No furniture at all. No carpet, either; just lots and lots of old newspaper and bits of cardboard – damp and smelly. Along one wall there were cages, stacked up on top of each other. Some were big enough for Willow to get into – others were much smaller. They were all empty... apart from one.

Willow was crouched low at the far corner, nose to nose through the bars with a tiny black creature. She was making a low noise in her throat – not a growl – more of a grunt. It was a noise of comfort, Joe realised, as he crouched down next to her and swung the torch beam in. The creature instantly scuttled to the back of the cage, whimpering.

'Hey! It's OK!' said Joe. 'We're here to rescue you!' He peered closer and saw it was a small dog, black and hairy, with a dainty black nose, high pointed ears and glittering dark eyes. There seemed to be purple dye on the fur on its back. Around its neck was a collar with a small silver disc on it. Squinting, Joe could make out what was engraved on it. KIZZY.

'Kizzy!' he gasped, putting his hand on Willow's head. 'That's one of your friends from the park, isn't it? I heard she'd gone missing!'

Willow nodded and looked up at him. The question in her eyes was quite clear. What are you going to do about this, Joe?!

Joe shone the torch back to the front of the cage, feeling for a catch. He found it quickly... but he also found another padlock. 'No!' He set the torch down, angled towards the cage, and began to test the lock in his fingers. This one wasn't rusty, but it was firmly closed. It had a keyhole, not a combination. He grabbed the torch and flashed it around the room – where would the keys be kept? There was a fireplace with a mantelpiece, but nothing on it except a thick layer of dust. The rest of the room was filled with more boxes and a few empty metal dog bowls on the floor. There was no sign of any keys.

Joe stood up. 'We have to get help,' he said to Willow. 'We can call the RSPCA or something.' Yes. Yes, that seemed like a sensible idea; the kind of thing Mum would say. Although Mum would never crawl through a window into a stranger's bungalow in the middle of the night. He would have to tell her what he and Willow had done... or maybe just make an anonymous call. He could do that maybe... or...

Before he could think of any other ideas there was a sudden shaft of red light, gleaming through the windows. There were no curtains – there didn't need to be because most of the front window was covered with ivy – but the light got through and made Willow's eyes glimmer like ruby discs. And there was noise, too... engine noise. Joe suddenly realised a van was backing towards the house and stopping just outside the gate.

Willow stood up and gave a low growl and Kizzy began to whimper more loudly. Joe's heart started to pound. He heard the engine drop to an idle and then the car door open. He heard voices – a man saying: 'Well – how was I to know you had another one in there? Oh keep your 'air on! I'm going to get it now, aren't I?'

Joe froze. Willow froze too. Now there were footsteps coming towards the bungalow; now there was the sound of a key turning in the front door; now the door was opening.

And there was nowhere to run.

# Chapter 18

# RUN!

'It's HIM,' Kizzy tells me and she's so scared, I catch it. Now I am so scared my bones are shaking.

'Run!' says Kizzy. 'RUN or he'll get you!'

But I can't run away and leave her. I will have to stay here and bite Smoky Lip Man on his purple hand. Except Joe is now dragging me away from Kizzy and back into the dark passage. 'Shhhhh!' he hisses. 'Shhhhh!' And I know why. There is a scratchy, clinky noise and a dark shadow through the glass of the door. But I don't get much chance to see anything because now we're back in the small room under the high window. Joe pulls me down onto the ground and whispers in my ear.

'Be quiet. Don't... make... a... sound.' He puts his arms around me and crouches down, pulling us behind the boxes. I can feel his heart beating fast; nearly as fast as mine.

The door to the house crashes open, just around the corner from where we hide, and a loud voice booms out: 'Where's the blinkin' light switch?' Feel curls plunge down the hallway and reach into our cupboard; they are dark and sour and angry.

This is not Smoky Lip Man – who smells just as bad but in a different way. Suddenly, yellow light throws itself across the ceiling and the man stomps up the hallway and then into the front room; I can tell by the sound and the smell. 'Where is it?!' grunts the man. Then he mutters and curses and there is the sound of metal on metal and the creak of a cage door being opened. Then a whimper and whine.

'Shaddup, you little rat,' says the man and Kizzy squeaks with terror. I leap up. It is time to bite. I never bite but I can bite and I've always known one day I might bite. The day is today. But Joe pulls me back down and hisses: 'NO! Stay still! Be quiet!' in my ear. I am knotted up inside. Everything in my body is yelling 'GO! BITE! BITE THE MAN!' but a small space in my head is saying 'No. Joe is right. The man might hurt Joe, too. You have to protect Joe, too.'

And by now it's too late anyway because the lights go out, the front door slams shut and Kizzy is gone. The van drives away. Joe gets up and runs into the front room to peer through the window. 'It's gone,' he says as I follow and leap up to put my paws on the sill. They've taken your friend,' he says. He looks at me and says: 'But I think I know where they've taken her. Come on. We've got to get out of here and find her.'

Getting out is easier than getting in because Joe just opens the front door. We run outside and back to the street where the bike is still leaning on a lamppost. The feel curls from the men in the van are still in the air, although they're fading fast. They drop and sag like something rotten.

'It's a bit of a ride,' says Joe as he switches the bike lights on again. 'And it's uphill. Can you keep up?'

I snort at him. Keep up? He'd better keep up with me.

# Chapter 19

## Granby Woods

Joe had never ridden his bike so fast. He realised, as they tore up the steep slope of Granby Way, that he'd also never been so angry. He was furious that anyone could keep dogs in cages and treat them badly. And he was scared, too – scared of whatever was happening up in Granby Woods. Because he was now quite certain that something very bad was happening in Granby Woods.

His sister seemed to agree. She was running way ahead of him, in just the same direction he was planning to cycle. It was as if she could read his mind. Or maybe she could smell the direction the van, with her little dog friend inside, had travelled.

Maybe this was a gang of dognappers, all meeting up in the woods to sell their stolen dogs to the kind of people who bought stolen dogs. Joe felt his heart beat a little faster – if it was possible for his heart to go any faster – as he pedalled up the hill, watching the shadowy black form of Willow bouncing about ten houses ahead of him.

'Willow!' he called. 'Slow down! You have to wait for me.'

At the top of the hill there was a T junction with the main road stretching off to his left and his right. Willow had already shot across it to the shadowy pathway on the other side which led down between high brick walls, towards the deeper darkness of Granby Woods. Joe glanced left and right; saw a car approaching on his right and then decided he didn't need to stop and wait for it. He pedalled even harder and shot out across the road and just as he reached the far kerb he noticed a flash of blue light and heard a whoop-whoop noise.

The jolt that went through him nearly toppled him sideways into the brick pillar beside the footpath. He'd just been whooped by a POLICE PATROL CAR! Joe glanced over his shoulder and, beneath the plastic peak of his bike helmet, saw the car pull across from the other side of the road and glide towards the kerb just behind him. NO! He couldn't get stopped by the police! Willow had already run ahead down the footpath to the woods and he might lose her while he tried to explain what he was doing out at this late hour. He couldn't lose her!

Joe took a sharp breath and then whacked his foot down on the pedal and shot away into the gloom of the footpath.

'HEY!' called out a commanding voice behind him. 'STOP! You've got no back light!'

He heard footsteps on the path but they were soon lost in the whoosh of the air past his ears and his hard, fast breathing, as he sped away, straining his eyes to see Willow. In the thin yellow beam of his front light (which was still working) he could make out the movement of her high flag of a tail. 'Willow!' he yelled. 'Willow! Emily! Wait for me!'

At last she slowed to a halt, turning to gaze back down the path at him; her round brown eyes gleaming silver as they reflected his bike lamp. She was trembling with agitation as she waited for him to catch up. Joe skidded to a halt and glanced back, fearfully. He half expected to see a policeman running after them – but there was nothing but shadow. Turning back, he realised the concrete footpath ended here and the thin, winding route through the trees into Granby Woods began. He couldn't ride along it; there was a wooden stile blocking the path. He could climb over it and Willow could duck down and crawl beneath it, but there was no way he could get the bike over it – and even if he could, the path was too narrow and knuckled up with tree roots for cycling. With a sigh, Joe leant the bike to the side of the stile and locked it to a thick plank with his chain.

'Time to go on foot,' he said. Willow nodded.

'Are we mad?' he added. 'Coming out here on our own in the middle of the night?'

Willow nodded again. And then rolled her eyes exactly the way she used to back when she was Emily.

Joe laughed, even though he was feeling really scared. He dug his hand into his jeans pocket and brought out a silver pen torch that he'd got for Christmas. The light from it was blueish white and quite powerful. He shone it into the woods and the trunks of trees suddenly snapped into view, like white fingers reaching up out of the soil. A few moths circled in the warm night air, dazed by the sudden glare. Joe angled the beam downwards at the path, partly so he and Willow could see where they were walking and not trip over any roots or rocks but also because he realised the light might be seen glinting through the trees... and whoever was already in Granby Woods, he didn't want to give away that he and Willow were there too.

He wondered if the bike hat might help if someone jumped out from behind a tree and hit him on the head. But as they walked on, nobody jumped out from behind anything. The blue light at his feet picked out a small rodent scurrying into some leaves – but that seemed to be the only other thing moving around out here.

Joe began to get the prickly feeling that he had just been a colossal idiot, coming up here with Willow. There was nobody else here. What was he doing? He should be tucked up in bed at home. And his sister should be in her basket, dreaming of rabbits. Did she dream of rabbits?

'Willow,' he murmured, thinking that talking might make him feel less scared. 'Do you dream about rabbits?'

Willow glanced up at him, her black nose shining in the torchlight, and rolled her eyes again as if to say Really! You ask me this NOW? And then she gave a little sigh and nodded.

'I think maybe we should... go home,' muttered Joe, coming to a halt. 'I don't think there's anyone here.' But Willow suddenly stood very still, her nose lifting and her ears moving forward. The low sound which came out of her made the hairs on Joe's neck stand up.

It was a deep, menacing growl.

# Chapter 20

## Twenty Quid: Five Minutes

One minute there is nothing but the small furry things in the leaves and the moths that spin past my nose. Nothing else. And then suddenly the wind changes and it's ALL coming at me. Feel curls flood over me like a tidal wave. They are long and tangled and sour. There is fear and anger and excitement and a darkness which is much darker than the dark I can see. I smell Smoky Lip Man and the man who came to get Kizzy. There are other men too; I don't know them but I already know I don't like them.

I run up through the river of feel curls and my warning is already rolling across my teeth; I can bite. I CAN bite. I CAN BITE AND I WILL BITE IF I HAVE TO.

Then I hear Joe cry out: 'WILLOW! SHHHH! WAIT! Wait for me!' and I realise I cannot just run and bite because I have to look after my brother too. He catches up and grabs my collar. 'Slowly and quietly,' he whispers, holding the light very small by our feet. 'Take me to them slowly and quietly. They mustn't know we're here.'

Of course. We must stalk. I lower my head and place my paws quietly. The feel curls are thicker and darker and more tangled and now I can hear crying. My kind… crying. Also… my kind making another noise, which I am not quite sure about. There is a shake in my inners. I am scared. But I am angry too. I want to let off such a yell. I want to lift my head and open my jaws and bawl out: 'I AM HERE AND I AM COMING AND I WILL BITE ANYONE WHO IS HURTING YOU! THEY WILL FEEL MY CLAWS AND THEY WILL FEEL MY JAWS! I WILL MAKE THEM CRY! I WILL SEE THEM OFF! SEE THEM OFF!'

But Joe is here, his hand on my collar, and he's whispering: 'Quiet, Willow. Quiet, Emily. Quiet now…'

There is light now. A glow like the moon – except this moon is on a long pole, half as high as the trees. It shines down into a shape like my food bowl. A big round bowl is made of mud and twigs, a circle between the trees. Metal criss-cross is all around it. Around the bowl stand men. Men with smoking paper on their lips and bottles in their hands, leaning over the criss-cross. There is paper in their hands too. They wave the paper around. They are laughing and happy but not really laughing and not really happy. The darkest, worst feel curls come from these men.

Then there is a cry and I see her. Kizzy comes out. She is dropped over the criss-cross and stands, shaking, in the middle of the bowl. The men start laughing and waving money and one of them says: 'Twenty quid!'

Another one says: 'Five minutes!'

# Chapter 21

## Croc

Joe crouched low behind some brambles, just beneath the slanted trunk of an old oak tree, and stared at the crowd of men. They stood around the circle of chicken wire, which someone had staked into the ground in the middle of the clearing to make a pen. They'd set up a lamp which bathed

the scene with light. This must be the dog sale, he realised. People were coming to buy stolen dogs. A short distance from the pen he could see four wooden crates with rope handles. He could make out the flash of frightened eyes inside the crates and he could hear whimpering.

He gritted his teeth, imagining how upset the owners of these dogs would be if they knew; how upset they must be already with their beloved pets gone missing. Then the little dog he and Willow had tried to rescue was suddenly dropped into the pen and stood there, trembling.

'Twenty quid!' said one of the men, holding up some notes.

Is that all? thought Joe. All of this… the dognapping and the sneaking around the woods in the night… for just twenty quid?

But then another man laughed and said: 'Five minutes. I give it five minutes.'

'Nah,' said the other one, 'these little terriers are well fierce. It'll last ten minutes, I reckon.'

'Against Croc?' laughed the man from the bungalow. 'You got to be jokin'. Croc will eat that in sixty seconds. It's just a warm up for the others.'

Joe wrapped his arms around Willow and took a long, slow breath. He was suddenly feeling sick and dizzy. He was beginning to understand what these men had come for. It wasn't to buy dogs at all. It was to watch dogs fight. And to bet on which dog would win… and which dog…

Joe pulled Willow further back into the trees with him. He had to do something. He had to stop this – NOW! But how? What could one boy and one labradoodle DO?

Now there was a lot of excitement around the pen. One end of it was being opened up and a growling, squat creature was being brought in on a tight leash by the man from the bungalow. It had a flat brown face and a row of jagged lower teeth and its eyes glittered red as it emerged through the dark. It was growling and pulling hard against its leash, dribble hanging from the corners of its mouth. Willow's friend ran to the far side of the pen and crouched against it as the dog they called Croc bared its sharp canines and snarled. The men hooted with laughter.

Joe didn't know what else to do. He climbed up the slanted trunk of the oak tree, shone his torch down from above and then, in as deep a voice as he could make, he bawled: 'STOP! POLICE!'

Even as he said it, he realised this was very possibly the stupidest thing he had ever done in his life. The crowd of men suddenly stopped talking and waving cash about and stared up into the branches, mouths gaping.

Joe knew the beam of his torch was pretty bright. They wouldn't be able to see him. He had sort of hoped the voice from the tree and the flare of his torch light might make them all scatter and run, leaving the dogs behind.

But instead they just peered up at him. The bungalow man, still holding onto Croc, called up: 'Police? Oh yeah? You sound a bit young to be a policeman, sonny. What are you doing up there?'

Joe gripped the branch and tried to stop the beam from his torch shaking. Below him he could see Willow moving in an agitated circle and prayed that she wouldn't leap out into view. 'Alright,' he said. 'I'm not police. But I have called them.

They're on their way. I filmed you all on my phone and I've sent the film to them. They know what you look like!'

Bungalow Man rubbed his greasy hair and looked around at the others, grinning. 'What do you think, boys? Should we be worried?'

There were sniggers and someone said: 'Get him down from there. Let's take a look at him.'

'I'm warning you,' Joe called down, wishing his voice would stop wobbling. 'This is all being filmed… it's streaming live back to the police right now!'

'What… from the middle of Granby Woods?' snorted Bungalow Man. 'There's no mobile phone signal out here, lad. You're bluffing.'

And then they stormed the tree and dragged him out of it.

# Chapter 22

# The Wild Way

Every dog has a wolf inside. We keep the wolf secret but we know it is there. One day the wolf may have to come out. Today is the day.

As the men pull Joe from the tree I throw myself at them with my claws and my teeth. For a few wild seconds I taste their skin and their fear. And then one kicks me in the side and I skid backwards through the brambles. My ears are ringing but I hear Joe shout out: 'NO! WILLOW! RUN! GET HELP!'

I want to protect my little brother! But I know humans well – better than my dog friends know them, because I was a human not so long ago. I am scared for Joe but I think maybe they won't dare to set Croc on a boy. So I must run for help. But…

…I scramble to my paws and run around the far side of the circle. I hear Kizzy whimper and see Croc. He is still in the bowl with her, being held back by Smoky Lip Man, who is watching the others bring Joe from the tree. Croc is telling Kizzy he is going to eat her as soon as he is off the leash. He is not pretending. This is not a game fight like we all have together up in the high park. Croc's wolf is not hidden. It never hides.

So I do what I can do, so easily. I leap over the criss-cross and into the bowl. Kizzy runs to me and I put down my head and make a bridge from the ground. My tail is against the criss-cross. Smoky Lip Man is only looking at Joe so he doesn't see, even though Croc is barking and snarling and pulling towards us. By the time Smoky Lip Man turns around, Kizzy has run up my head, shoulders and back and leapt over the criss-cross. I turn, growl back at Croc for a second, and then leap over after her.

'STOP THOSE DOGS!' yells Smoky Lip Man, but he is too late. All the men went to get Joe and they are on the other side. Kizzy shoots away into the dark trees and I follow her. There are more shouts and lights coming after us, but they will never catch us. We head deep into the tunnels in the tangles made by foxes and badgers – low and winding and no good for humans. This is the wild way. This is where they cannot follow.

I am filled with so much feel. I feel joy because Kizzy has escaped and we are running away. Nothing can be better than being with a dog friend and running away. Except being with a human you love. These are feels which fight each other. How can a dog have joy for running away AND joy for running back?

Now, though, it's not just feels of joy. FEAR is really strong. I MUST save Joe from Smoky Lip Man and his pack. I must run home to Jed and Granny and tell them everything. I tell Kizzy this as we run through the tangle tunnels. She is running with joy too but she understands what I fear and what I must do. We run for the town, for our homes, together. And then Kizzy asks me how I will tell everything to Jed and Granny. Because… we can't tell everything. We can only give clues.

I stop running to think. When I get home what will happen? I will get told off and cuddled and then told off a bit more and then… put to bed. The doors will be locked. There will be nothing else I can do to help Joe. I cannot go home.

But… I can go to my old home… I have to go back to Mum.

# Chapter 23

# Caged

'What are we going to do with him?'

The men stood in a ring around him, staring down and shuffling about. Some of them looked worried.

'We can't let him go,' said Bungalow Man. 'He's seen what's going on. He'll run straight to the police.'

'We should pack up,' said another man. 'We can do this somewhere else.'

There were grunts and grumbles and someone said: 'There's nowhere better than here. This took weeks to set up. I'm not running off home because of some snotty-nosed kid.'

'We've got another three dogs for Croc,' said the man from the bungalow. 'I say we put the kid in a crate and get on with it.'

'He'll still run and tell, as soon as we let him go,' said another man, in a low, menacing voice. Joe couldn't see his face under the peak of the cap he wore, just the red glow of his cigarette as he sucked on it.

Bungalow Man crouched down and stared at Joe. 'No, he won't,' he said. 'I know where that dog lives. I've marked it out already. You listen to me, sonny,' he went on, narrowing his eyes. 'We're going to have a bit of sport up here, that's all. There's no law against having a bit of fun.'

'Yeah, there is,' argued a man in a furry hood. 'That's why we do it here.'

'Yeah, alright, Phil!' spat Bungalow Man. 'It's a figure of speech. What I mean is, we're not doing anyone any harm.'

'Apart from the dogs,' pointed out furry hood man. 'We're definitely harming the dogs.'

'I'll harm you if you don't put a sock in it!' warned Bungalow Man. Then he shook his head and went on. 'You can just stay put in the crate and when we're done, we'll let you go,' he said. 'And then you'll go home to your mummy and you won't say a THING about it – because if you do, that labradoodle will be gone in 24 hours. Trust me. I'll have it. And then Croc will have it for dinner.' Croc, held nearby by one of Bungalow Man's dog fighting mates, gave a phlegmy growl to underline this. 'But as long as you say nothing, that dog will always be safe. You get me?'

Joe didn't say anything. There was nothing he could say which would make this any better. He just gritted his teeth as they grabbed him by his arms and propelled him across to the crates and shoved him inside the biggest one, which had housed Croc before he'd been let out. It was grimy and sticky beneath his hands and knees and smelt of old meat and fish. It was only just big enough for him to crouch in. Someone slammed the front shut and Joe could only stare out between the metal bars. In the crate next to him he could make out the wet nose of what looked like a spaniel. He didn't need to have dog senses to smell how scared the spaniel was. Joe screwed

87

his eyes tight shut. This was a disaster. All he had done was find out what was going on up in Granby Woods and then get himself caught. He was going to have to stay here while the dogfights happened and there was nothing he could do to stop them. He WOULD go to the police, of course... but if he did... his sister was a marked dog. Would it be better to pretend he hadn't seen anything?

And maybe this was all a trick anyway. Maybe they were never going to let him go at all...

The only good thing he could cling to was that Willow and her friend Kizzy had managed to escape. And maybe... just maybe... they could get help.

Oh come on, Joe, said a cold voice in his head. This isn't a Disney movie. Willow might be Emily and Emily might be brilliant and amazing... but she still can't explain what's going on.

Someone came and got the spaniel and Joe covered his ears and screwed his eyes shut.

# Chapter 24

# Understanding

The way home is easy – I can smell it. Kizzy wants to run straight home too but she stays with me because she knows I need her. And she knows the other dogs need her. There are three other dogs who have been stolen from other places.

It's very late and most of the humans are in their homes now. We see a fox by a bin as we run; the fox lifts its snout and wants to know what's going on. I send it a message in feel curls – bad men in the woods; hurting dogs. Stay away! The fox flashes his tail and I realise it is HIM. But I cannot stay to tell him more.

As we reach my road I have to slow down. I have to be careful. If Jed or Granny see me come back they will take me indoors and I will not be able to help Joe. I have to get to my old mum – Joe's mum – and make her understand that Joe is in danger.

We creep low along the wall outside Jed and Granny's house. Kizzy whimpers when she smells the purple on the wall. This is the mark of Smoky Lip Man and I now know what it means. It means DOG HERE I WANT TO STEAL.

I shiver and we creep on, to the gate into Joe's house. It is not quite shut so I boop it open with my nose and we creep up to the front step and look at the front door. The house is quiet but there is a light on in the hallway and the front room. I can smell that Mum is in there. Her feel curls are calm. She does not know Joe is out in the woods, in danger. She thinks he is up in his room.

I could bark… but if I bark Granny or Jed will come out. So I cannot bark.

There is a little circle in a square up on the wall next to the door. I know what this is and how to work it. If I was Kizzy sized it would be no good, but I am tall and I can do this. I jump up and paw against the circle in the square. It doesn't work. I try again. It doesn't work. I try again.

And it DOES work. A bell chimes inside the house. We sit and wait. And then the door opens and Mum stares down at us and says: 'Willow? What are you doing here at this time of night? And… who's this?!'

I don't wait for her to ask me anything else I can't answer. I push past her and run into the house and gallop up the stairs. Kizzy follows. Mum is shouting: 'Willow! WHAT do you think you're DOING? You'll wake Joe up!' And she's coming right up after me, which is good because it's what she needs to do. I jump at Joe's door and scrape it with my claws – so does Kizzy. 'WHAT ON EARTH?' yells Mum and then my claws catch the handle and the door opens and we tumble in. And then we turn and look at her because the bed is empty and now she knows Joe ISN'T HERE.

She goes very quiet. And then she runs to check the bathroom. And then she starts shouting: 'JOE!' all over the house and we sit and wait until she comes back. She gets down on her knees and her face is like a pebble – white and still. She says: 'Willow… where is Joe?'

We are just about to show her when the doorbell chimes again. We all run down the stairs. 'Wait there!' says Mum and opens the door.

'Juliet,' says a man.

'Ben!' says Mum.

'You'll probably think I'm nuts,' says this Ben. 'And he's probably tucked up in bed… but I could've sworn I saw Joe out on his bike up by Granby Woods about half an hour ago.'

This Ben is the man who was in the car that nearly ran over my little brother! Mum stares at him and then stares at me and Kizzy and says: 'I think these two just came to tell me the same thing!'

Ben drops down onto his knees and looks at us. He stares hard at Kizzy's fur. 'It's purple,' he says.

'Um… yes…' squeaks Mum and flaps her hands about. 'So?!'

'There's purple spray paint on the wall next door,' says Ben. He stares at me and Kizzy for a few seconds. 'Oh no,' he says.

'What?!' says Mum. 'What's going on?!'

'You see spray paint on front garden walls sometimes,' says Ben. 'It's a marker… it means someone has seen something in the house they want to come back for. Like…'

'…a dog?' says Mum. 'Dognappers?'

I bark and nod my head.

'Did she just… nod?' asks Ben, looking astonished.

I can't wait around all night. I push past Ben and run back down the path with Kizzy close behind me. I stop at the gate and stare off in the direction we just came from. I bark three times and then I lift my paw and try to point. The door opens at my house and Jed comes out.

'Willow?' he says. 'What are you doing over there? I thought you were out in the garden.' He looks embarrassed. 'Sorry, Juliet,' he says. 'She's been outside for ages. Sometimes I'm watching telly and I forget to let her back in. Come on, Willow. Oh – who's your friend?'

I shake my head and bark again and then Ben says: 'We need Willow's help, Jed. Joe has gone missing. I think she's trying to take us to him.'

Then things start to move very fast. Another man is in a car and it has a whirly blue light on it. Ben puts me and Kizzy in the back of the car with Mum and Jed – and then we speed off back to Granby Woods.

I just hope it's not too late.

# Chapter 25

## Scream

Joe could hear the men cheering in spite of his hands over his ears. The dogfight must have started. His insides crunched up and he felt sick but he couldn't help looking out through the bars. Then a flash of red fur went past. A large fox slunk along behind the crowd and then turned and shook its tail, sending out a spray of stinky fox scent which rose like steam and drifted through the golden light over the pit.

Suddenly the growling from Croc turned into a ferocious, wild barking. The fox ran around the circle of men, lifted its head and then let out the most blood-chilling scream Joe had ever heard. The men froze and then turned to stare at it in amazement.

'It's a blinkin' fox!' one of them cried out.

'Now THAT'S something worth betting on,' said another.

The fox screamed again and Croc went so crazy he threw himself against the pen. There were more shouts and then a crunch and the dog was free and chasing the fox – which vanished into the dark in an instant. Croc let out a howl of fury and galloped after it while Bungalow Man yelled: 'WAIT!

Stop him!' But it was too late – Croc had already bolted deep into the undergrowth, leaving the poor shivering spaniel alone in the broken pen.

Go! thought Joe. Run away NOW while you can!

But someone grabbed it before it could move and then there was another shout from the men who'd chased after Croc. With much snarling and whining, Croc was caught and wrestled back to the clearing.

'This is some entertainment!' said furry hooded man, swigging from a brown bottle. 'What next, eh?'

'Come on,' shouted someone else. 'Get Croc onto the spaniel! We 'aven't got all night!'

Croc was put back inside the pen and pointed in the direction of the spaniel, which was pressed up against the chicken wire, whimpering and huddled into a ball of fear. Croc began to snarl and lurch towards it, held back by his collar while a cheer went up around the pen.

Joe pressed his hands over his ears and screwed his eyes shut. He couldn't bear to watch.

Then there was a big flare of light. From three directions there were loud shouts. 'STOP! STAY WHERE YOU ARE! POLICE!' This time it sounded nothing like a boy.

Swearing and hissing, the men began to scramble away, trying to hide themselves in the trees, but they didn't get far. Six or seven officers in reflective jackets were closing in – along with one very bouncy woolly dog who ran straight through the chaos and slammed up against the crate. The force knocked the clip off the lock and the front opened. Joe crawled out just in time to kick a leg out and trip Bungalow Man over as he tried to run past with Croc. The man fell head first into the roots of a tree and then Croc, twisting off his lead, sank his teeth into his owner's leg and ran off into the woods.

Then Willow ran across and bit Bungalow Man's bum.

# Chapter 26

## The Penny Drops

The smell of meat and sugar and metal is as good today as it ever was when I was Emily, watching from my chair.

As a special treat, Joe has been allowed to take me into The Gold Rush with him. He asked Lisa, the lady who works there, and she said yes, because she's seen my picture in the paper. We are famous. The paper came through the door today and Jed held it up to show me the picture of us and said: 'Look at the headline, Willow! You're front page news! Listen - SCHOOLBOY AND LABRADOODLE FOIL DOGFIGHT GANG!'

So I have had LOTS of chicken sticks and cuddles and now I'm even allowed to come into The Gold Rush and watch as Joe plays the Penny Falls.

'Did you really both fight off a gang of dognappers?' says Lisa, playing with my ears as Joe puts the coins in. They rattle and ping down past the pins and spin across the shelf.

'Well… Willow fought them off mostly,' says Joe. 'She bit the ringleader in the bum. But we both tracked them down in the woods… and then Ben, our policeman friend, he saw me out on my bike so he knew sort of where I was and then Willow and Kizzy showed him the way to exactly where. They got there just in time to stop the dogfight and arrest everyone.'

'How did you know they were there?' asks Lisa.

'I didn't,' says Joe. 'Willow knew. She ran off and I just followed her.' He doesn't look at Lisa because his face is going pink. He's not a good fibber. He had to fib to Ben and Mum, too... because they would never believe the real story. We think they believe him. Probably.

'Did they catch them all?' asks Lisa, as some pennies fall over the edge and land in the big metal pocket at the bottom.

'Yeah, they did,' says Joe. 'Even Croc, the fighting dog. Ben radioed for back-up. The police surrounded them. They're all going to jail, I hope.'

'You're a local hero!' says Lisa. 'Everyone will be stopping you in the street!'

'Not for long,' says Joe and suddenly those old, sad feel curls are tipping out of him and tumbling to the floor like the pennies in the falls.

'Why's that then?' says Lisa.

'We're leaving,' says Joe. 'Mum has to sell the house. We can't afford it. We've got to move into a little flat right on the other side of town.'

Lisa smiles and pats his shoulder. 'Well, you never know. Maybe you'll like it over there,' she says, and walks off.

Joe scoops up some pennies he's tipped out of the falls and then pokes them all back in until there are none left. 'Come on, Willow,' he says. 'Better go home. I promised Mum I'd start packing up my room. And then I've got to help with your old room.'

And that's when I remember.

Thing 3.

# Chapter 27

# WOOF!

Joe was just about to leave The Gold Rush when Willow started going crazy. She suddenly lurched out down the steps onto the boardwalk and started dragging him along on the end of the lead.

'What are you doing, Em?' he spluttered, nearly losing his footing. 'Emily! I mean… Willow!' (Was he ever going to get used to this?) 'Slow down!' She did slow down a bit but she kept trotting along at a very fast pace, her flaggy tail waving at speed and her pink tongue rippling across her teeth as she kept staring up at him. Every so often she would make a little excited noise – half wuff, half whine.

'What is up with you?' asked Joe, puffing as he ran along in step with her. But Willow just kept on wagging and wuffing and dragging him along. When they got to their street he tried to open her gate and take her in to Jed and Mrs Ellis's place, but she shook her head determinedly and pulled him along to his own gate, under the estate agent's sign, which now read SOLD – SUBJECT TO CONTRACT. Joe winced as he saw it. He winced every time he saw it. He hated that sign.

He had talked to Jed about coming over to see Willow and take her out after they had moved, even though he'd have to take two buses to get there.

'You're welcome, mate,' Jed had said, but he'd looked doubtful. 'I mean – any time – but how often are you going to be able to come over, really? What with your new flat and your new school and stuff. Willow's really going to miss you.'

Joe took a deep breath as he got Willow to sit down so he could unlatch the gate. There was no point in letting it get to him. He was going to take two buses across town – at least three times a week. As long as Mum could afford to give him the bus fare. And if she couldn't… well, then, he would come over on his bike… if Mum would let him. He bit his lip; fairly sure that Mum wouldn't let him. It was a long way on very busy roads. OK – so he would walk. It would take nearly two hours but he would do it. He couldn't lose his sister again, not when he'd only just found her.

As soon as the gate was open, Willow burst through it and up to the front door.

'Look… you can't stay for long,' Joe said. 'I've got to help with the packing and you… you'll just get in the way. You know you will.'

Willow looked up at him innocently. Then his sister winked. Literally winked. It made him laugh out loud. As soon as he opened the door Willow shot inside and then he had to come over all stern and make her sit at the foot of the stairs while he undid the lead. He could feel excited energy thrumming through her doggy frame.

'Is that you, Joe?' called down Mum, already upstairs, packing.

'No – it's a burglar,' called back Joe. 'And the burglar's dog.'

'Really, there isn't time for playing with Willow,' Mum said.

'I know – I'll take her back in a minute,' said Joe. 'I just –'

Then – POW! She was off again, straight up the stairs and onto the landing. Joe heard Mum shout 'WILLOW!' and then there was a scratch and a thud as the dog bashed open the door to Emily's room.

'It's OK, Mum,' said Joe, charging up the stairs and onto the landing. 'I'll sort her out.'

But as soon as he stepped into Emily's room he saw that Willow was sitting quietly on the bedside rug, looking as good as gold. Mum leant around the door and sighed, reaching over to scratch Willow's woolly head. 'She can stay if she sits quietly,' she said. 'Just to keep you company while you sort out the books and stuff.'

'OK,' said Joe. 'You'll be quiet, won't you, Willow?'

Mum blinked. 'Did she just nod?'

Joe laughed, slightly nervously. 'Yeah, she does seem to do that sometimes.'

Mum went back to sorting out her room and Joe closed the door and just sat and looked at Willow for a few seconds.

'Is this weird for you?' he said, glancing around the room. 'Me… packing up all your old stuff like you're not around any more?'

Willow rolled her eyes and jumped onto the bed.

'No!' hissed Joe. 'You're meant to sit quietly!'

But Willow was now grabbing the pillows in her teeth and throwing them onto the floor and then digging her paws down between the mattress and the padded material headboard. Her tail was going frantically and she was making little urgent growls.

'What are you doing?! STOP IT!' Joe tried to drag her away by the collar but she would not stop. She tumbled sideways off the bed and then grabbed the top corner of the mattress in her strong jaws and began to pull it right off the bed.

He grabbed her around her furry waist and dragged her along the carpet, grunting: 'Cut it out or I'm taking you next door NOW!'

And then she stopped struggling, wiggled around to face him, jumped up and put her warm paws on his shoulders and stared right into his face, panting. There was something in her expression he couldn't quite work out. And then he said: 'Willow… Emily… Are you trying to find something?'

Willow nodded very clearly – three times.

'Is it… behind the bed?'

She nodded again.

'Well… why didn't you say so?' Joe got up and pulled the heavy metal and wood bedstead away from the wall. Old comics, an empty Maltesers packet, an ancient dusty sock and a book called Woof! were wedged along the skirting board where the bed had been.

Willow immediately foraged through these items, pausing to sneeze once over the sock and then stood back for a while, staring at them, her ears tipped forward and her nose twitching.

'Well… what's so important about your old sock?' asked Joe. 'Or did you want me to read to you?' He picked up the book. 'Like I used to.' He felt his throat go a bit tight and thick as he remembered reading to Emily. He'd read this book to her – about a boy who turns into a dog – just a week before she'd died.

It was only when she licked his face that he realised a tear or two had leaked out. 'It's OK,' he said. 'I will come back to see you, I promise.'

Then Willow turned and started to beat up the wall.

# Chapter 28

# Thing 3

I remember bits of my last day as Emily. I was feeling floaty. But sometimes, when Mum came in to talk to me and stroke my face, I came back down for a bit. I could squeeze her hand. I was even looking at the book. Joe had finished reading it to me but I didn't want to let it go. I liked the story and wanted to keep it in my head.

There was something I needed to show Mum. Or show Joe when he got home. It was under my pillow. An exciting thing. A little square, shiny, exciting thing. I should have shown them before but I kept floating up and forgetting.

While Mum had gone to make a cup of tea I moved my hand behind my head and under the pillow and pulled the shiny square thing out. It took a very long time because my hands, back then, did not do as they were told very much.

But I got it. It was in my hand. I held it up in the sunlight and its numbers shone. They were very special. And then I dropped it. It fell behind my head and I never saw it fall. I was floating again... and this time, I didn't float back down, even when Mum came back in. I just kept floating up and up and that was the last I saw of the shiny square thing or the book. Or anything, as Emily.

I make Joe sit. And stay. And then I go to the wall. There is a square white thing on the wall where the end of the bed was. It has air coming through it and I can smell Jed outside in our garden. It is a small window, not for light, but for feel curls to get through. There is a tiny gap along the top where it meets the wall and I can see a corner of silver. Carefully, carefully, I put out my tongue and press it hard against the corner and slowly lick up the wall. It comes up with my tongue. I lick it right along the wall, away from the gap. And then I let it drop to the floor.

'What have you got there?' whispers Joe. He's stopped sitting and is now on his hands and knees, right next to me.

I look at the silvery thing and I remember the numbers. I carried this all the way home from The Gold Rush, the day before I started floating. And I forgot about it until I found it by the bed. It was hard to make my fingers work, but I did. I did it with my nails. My old Emily nails.

Joe picks it up and stares at it. And then his face goes very red. And then he starts to breathe like he's just run around the high park with me and Loki.

'One hundred thousand!' he breathes. 'ONE HUNDRED THOUSAND!' He starts waving it high in the air and yelling: 'MUM! MUUUUM!'

Mum comes rushing in, looking scared, and Joe starts jumping around the room.

'It's the scratch card! It's Emily's scratch card! It WON! It won the BIG money! MUUUUM!'

Mum grabs it and stares at it, her face also going red. Then she shakes her head and grabs Joe's arm. 'Hang on… hang on sweetheart… this must be more than a year old. We might be too late to collect this.'

'NO!' Joe stands still and all the red goes out of his face.

Mum squishes up her eyes and then reads, slowly: 'August the 23rd… the last claim they will accept is… in two day's time! Joe! GET THE PHONE!'

# Chapter 29

## A Gift from Emily

Joe knew money wasn't everything… but it was a lot. After their phone call they got more phone calls from the Scratch Card Lottery people and then there was a special meeting at their house and forms were signed and someone opened a bottle of Champagne.

And then the money came through and on that day, Mum sent a nice card to the annoying estate agent, explaining that they no longer wanted to move and apologising for taking up his time. She put a £50 note in with it.

Then she and Joe went outside and kicked over the SOLD – SUBJECT TO CONTRACT sign.

'It's almost like a gift from Emily… from the afterlife,' Mum said, as they sat on the front step, looking at the toppled over sign. She didn't often talk about Emily and it was nice that she could say this without gulping.

'It is a gift from Emily,' said Joe. He heard a thud and two woolly paws arrived on top of the fence.

'And a gift from Willow too, of course,' said Mum. 'I still can't believe she just snuffled it out randomly from all the rubbish behind Emily's bed.'

Willow grinned at them, her tongue wobbling across her teeth.

'You know, I know it's daft,' said Mum, putting her arm around Joe's shoulders. 'But sometimes I really do feel like Emily is here with us.'

'I know what you mean,' said Joe. 'In fact, I'm pretty sure she's here right now…'

# About the Author

Ali Sparkes is the Blue Peter Award winning author of **Frozen In Time**, the acclaimed **Shapeshifter series**, UK National Children's Book Awards finalist **Car-Jacked**, Carnegie-nominated **Wishful Thinking** and more than 50 other titles.

A former BBC broadcast journalist and newspaper reporter, Ali has also written comedy for BBC Radio 4 and edited a successful BBC magazine.

Her books have been translated into dozens of languages and are well-loved in libraries and homes around the world.

# Acknowledgements

Many thanks to the Mayfield Park dogs and their humans for inspiration, advice... and the occasional spare poo bag.

Other books for young people available from Stairwell Books

| | |
|---|---|
| Ivy Elf's Magical Mission | Elisabeth Kelly |
| Pandemonium of Parrots | Dawn Treacher |
| The Pirate Queen | Charlie Hill |
| Harriet the Elephotamus | Fiona Kirkman |
| A Business of Ferrets | Alwyn Bathan |
| Shadow Cat Summer | Rebecca Smith |
| Very Bad Gnus | Suzanne Sheran |
| The Water Bailiff's Daughter | Yvonne Hendrie |
| Season of the Mammoth | Antony Wootten |
| The Grubby Feather Gang | Antony Wootten |
| Mouse Pirate | Dawn Treacher |
| Rosie and John's Magical Adventure | The Children of Ryedale District Primary Schools |

For further information please contact rose@stairwellbooks.com

www.stairwellbooks.co.uk
@stairwellbooks

Lightning Source UK Ltd.
Milton Keynes UK
UKHW010623110123
415159UK00001B/43